TALES FROM A VILLAGE SCHOOL

TALES FROM A
VILLAGE SCHOOL

MISS READ

ILLUSTRATIONS BY KATE DICKER

MICHAEL JOSEPH
LONDON

MICHAEL JOSEPH LTD

Published by the Penguin Group
27 Wrights Lane, London w8 5tz
Penguin Books Inc., 375 Hudson Street, New York, New York 10014, USA
Penguin Books Australia Ltd, Ringwood, Victoria, Australia
Penguin Books Canada Ltd, 10 Alcorn Avenue, Toronto, Ontario, Canada m4v 3b2
Penguin Books (NZ) Ltd, 182–190 Wairau Road, Auckland 10, New Zealand

Penguin Books Ltd, Registered Offices: Harmondsworth, Middlesex, England

First published in Great Britain September 1994
Second impression November 1994
Third impression December 1994

Filmset by Datix International Limited, Bungay, Suffolk
Printed in England by Clays Ltd, St Ives plc
Set in 11½/13½pt Monophoto Garamond

ISBN 0 7181 0070 0

Contents

Acknowledgements

The author gratefully acknowledges the publications (given in brackets below) in which these stories first appeared. Copyright in individual stories as follows:

'The Lucky Hole' © Miss Read 1953 (*Observer*); 'Eskimos in the Sand Tray' © Miss Read 1959 (*Times Educational Supplement (TES)*); 'Harvest Festival' © Miss Read 1953 (*TES*); 'School Dinner for Forty' © *Punch* 1950 (*Punch*); 'Michaelmas Fair' © Miss Read 1955 (*TES*); 'Damage by Conkers' © *Punch* 1952 (*Punch*); 'Conkers and Gingernuts' © Miss Read 1954 (*TES*); 'Gunpowder, Treason and Plot' © Miss Read 1954 (*TES*); 'Snurling' © *Punch* 1952 (*Punch*); 'Christmas Cards for Forty' © Punch 1949 (*Punch*); 'The Craftsman' © Miss Read 1954 (*TES*); 'Carols for Forty' © *Punch* 1952 (*Punch*); 'Forty in the Wings' © *Punch* 1951 (*Punch*); 'Sleigh Bells for the Village School' © Miss Read 1953 (*TES*); 'Snow on Their Boots' © Miss Read 1955 (*TES*); 'Odour of Sanctity' © Miss Read 1962 (*TES*); 'Winter Gloom' © Miss Read 1956 (*TES*); 'Unstable Element' © Miss Read 1956 (*TES*); 'Black Magic' © Miss Read 1958 (*TES*); 'Stiff Test for Forty' © *Punch* 1952 (*Punch*); 'The Visitor' © Miss Read 1954 (*TES*); 'Conflicting Evidence' © *The Countryman* 1956 (this essay first appeared in *The Countryman* magazine); 'Rain on my Desk' © Miss Read 1953 (*TES*); 'Thirty-one and a Donkey' © Miss Read 1953 (*Observer*); 'Economy for Forty' © *Punch* 1952 (*Punch*); 'The Real Thing' © Miss Read 1954 (*The Lady*); 'Nature Walk for Forty' © *Punch* 1949 (*Punch*); 'Wild Surmise' © *Punch* 1952 (*Punch*); 'Goldfish and Frogspawn' © Miss Read 1955 (*TES*); 'Eight-a-side Cricket' © Miss Read 1954 (*TES*); 'Night and Day' © Miss Read 1955 (*TES*); 'The Runaway' © Miss Read 1957 (*TES*); 'Borrow a Pound' © *Punch* 1951 (*Punch*); 'The Flag' © Miss Read 1955 (*TES*); 'Lost Property' © Miss Read 1957 (*TES*); 'PT for Forty' © *Punch* 1949 (*Punch*); 'Clerical Error' © Miss Read 1953 (*TES*); 'Afterglow' © Miss Read 1953 (*TES*); 'Soft and Hard Boiled' © Miss Read 1954 (*TES*); 'Last Day of Term' © Miss Read 1954 (*TES*).

Foreword

This collection of short stories is the direct result of my lifelong involvement with country schools.

I spent three happy years at a Kentish village school in the 1920s. Later in life, I had short spells of supply teaching at various Berkshire schools, which confirmed my own belief that a well-run village school is the ideal place for a young child to begin its education.

I always wanted to write and I am often asked how I started. My approach was practical rather than poetic, but as I would prefer to be Anthony Trollope rather than Percy Bysshe Shelley, it is possibly just as well.

I had always been attracted to the light essay, admiring its brevity, grace and wit, achieved by many writers from Hazlitt and Charles Lamb to the eminent essayists of my own youth such as Hilaire Belloc, A. A. Milne and E. V. Knox. The last two I came across mainly in *Punch*, which was one of the few magazines accepting such work when I began to write after the Second World War. I determined to get into *Punch*. Perhaps I was setting my sights too high for a beginner, but in time I achieved my purpose.

There was a more practical side to deciding to write light essays. Our young daughter was at school, and I had the house to myself. With any luck, I could draft an essay of 850 to 1,000 words in that time.

I also wrote short verses, not only for *Punch*, but for *The Lady*, *Country Life* and any other journal which seemed to welcome 'corner-fillers'.

This was in the early 1950s, when Kenneth Bird, better known as the brilliant cartoonist Fougasse, was editor of *Punch*. It was during his reign that I began to contribute more regularly with a series based on an infants' teacher's monologue, called 'The Forty Series'.

It had often occurred to me when I was teaching that a recording of the idiotic outpourings heard in the infants' room might be diverting. (Joyce Grenfell perfected this art.) I would hear myself saying: 'I'm looking for a well-behaved frog for our play, and three really trustworthy rabbits.' I wrote a number of such things, which *Punch* took. *Punch* also took several country school essays and 'Damage by Conkers' and 'Snurling', to be found in this collection, were among them.

The *Times Educational Supplement* also took a great many country school articles.

But perhaps I was most fortunate in appearing in *The Observer*. 'The Lucky Hole' came out in 1953 and led to an invitation from the publishing house of Michael Joseph to write my first book *Village School*, and to form a happy relationship with that publisher which has lasted forty years. 'Thirty One and a Donkey' a little later introduced me to a long spell of most interesting work for the BBC's Schools Programmes. Both stories are included in this volume.

Memories of my own Kentish village school and spells of supply teaching influenced my work greatly, as examples here show. Later, my novels about Fairacre and Thrush Green echoed the country school theme as well as my feeling for the changing seasons in the English countryside. These two interests, I believe, find a ready response in the majority of my readers and, after all, my aim is to entertain them.

I still value the light essay and feel happiest when employing it. It is, I believe, the perfect training for most types of writing, for it needs tailoring to a desired length, a strong begining and ending, and the power of holding the attention of the reader. It forces the writer to be brief, discriminating and alert to the response of his public.

I enjoyed writing these stories. I hope that others may enjoy reading them.

The Lucky Hole

The children first showed me the lucky hole when we were out for a nature walk. It was one of those pellucid afternoons of late autumn, when the bare fields stretching away beneath an immense sky remind one of Dutch landscapes. Far away, in the distance, stood a clump of yellow elm trees, for all the world like stumps of cauliflower in piccalilli.

We had skirted a ploughed field and were returning up the hill to the village, bearing hips and haws, travellers' joy, bryony and a few nuts and blackberries stuffed precariously into disgraceful handkerchiefs. As we approached the church the children broke into a run, close by the flint wall. They stopped in a bunch, John with his fingers inserted in the socket of a large grey flint.

'Miss, this is the lucky hole!' they explained excitedly.

'Sometimes there's a sweet in it!'

'Or nuts!'

'Eric found a penny once!'

'Who puts the things in?' I asked.

'Anybody as likes,' they said casually. 'Our mums, or us does ourselves. Then the next one finds it, see?'

We trudged on up to school, the sun dazzling our eyes. It was almost like summer, we agreed.

But winter came overnight. As I cycled the three miles to school next morning there was a cold mist and the grass was grey with frost. The dahlias, so brave yesterday, stood wet and brown in the cottage gardens. The mist grew thicker as I pushed up the downs, and by the time I reached the crossroads it was impossible to see more than a few yards ahead. Clammy and mysterious, the mist swirled across the lane.

'Here she is!' said a voice close by me, and two small figures appeared through the fog. Eric and John, who often met me near the school, had chosen this, of all mornings, to greet me two miles from their own village.

I looked at them with dismay. They had no overcoats, and wore thin grey flannel suits. Their legs and hands were mauve with the cold and their skimpy sandals sodden; but their eyelashes were glamorously festooned with mist and their gappy smiles were undimmed.

'We was a bit early,' they explained, 'so we just come along in case you was lost.'

Touched though I was by this solicitude, I was not going to be bamboozled by these blandishments.

'You know quite well,' I said, 'that you are not supposed to come beyond the church to meet me. I must go on because the others will be waiting, but you must follow as fast as you can.'

I remounted. 'Keep together!' I shouted back through the mist. 'And *run* . . . or you'll have shocking colds!'

'Goodbye, Miss, goodbye!' they called cheerfully. I could hear their feet pounding obediently in my wake, the sound growing fainter and fainter behind me.

It was getting much colder, and I was worried about them. It would take them over half an hour to get to school. I might, I thought remorsefully, have been a little kinder to the poor dears. They could have had my scarf, for one thing, and the dilapidated raincoat that was strapped to my bicycle. I imagined them falling exhausted by the lonely road; meeting mad bulls, escaped lunatics, and, worst of all, their own irate mothers.

By this time I was swerving along the flint wall which held the lucky hole. I felt in my pocket for a small paper bag containing a few sticky mint humbugs. Peering closely at the wall, I came at last to the yawning lucky hole. As one who brings a votive offering to the gods, I poked the bag into the gap. Perhaps, I told myself, the luck would work for both the giver and the receiver. At any rate, it was the least I could do to salve my pricking conscience; their last half-mile should have the solace of a sweet and bulging cheek.

At school we said our prayers, sang our hymn and learnt an encouraging snatch of psalm, while outside the trees dripped. The ancient clock on the wall said half past nine, and with some vague, unhappy recollections of first aid for those suffering from exposure, I tipped the children's milk into a saucepan and set it on the stove to warm. The children exchanged delighted glances. Winter had really come!

Surely, I thought, they should be here by now? Could they have lost their way? Fallen down? Gone home? Broken a leg? I could see the headlines in our local paper ... 'CALLOUS SCHOOLMISTRESS REPRIMANDED BY MAGISTRATE'. In another ten minutes, I told myself agitatedly, I must certainly ring for the police. I began to write up the seven-times table on the blackboard, with quick, distracted strokes, and, as I bent to write the last cramped line, I heard them. Never were children's footsteps more welcome!

'Miss,' they said as they burst in, bringing with them a trail of mist and an overpowering smell of mint humbugs, 'Miss, it was lovely out! And look what we found in that hole we showed you yesterday! Ain't that a real lucky hole, now, ain't it?'

Eskimos in the Sand Tray

Salting down beans and sledging with the Eskimos may seem to most housewives to have no connections at all. For those of us, however, who have taught young children and have also this summer frugally stored the fruits of our gardens, the two subjects are inextricably associated. From the moment we grasp the block of salt in our left hand and raise the kitchen knife in our right, time dissolves, and we are twenty years back.

Those were the days! Against Geography in our weekly record book 'Life among the Eskimos' appeared for three or four weeks, and the ingenuity and physical labour that lay behind the laconic entry was staggering. In the first place a gripping account had to be given of the winter's cold, the months-long night, the clothing, diet, home conditions and general deportment of the Eskimos. This, in itself, was no light task with children of six and seven years of age, for, as well as a suitably simple vocabulary and an arresting style of narration, superhuman patience was needed to maintain a coherent account in the teeth of such interruptions as: 'I've been and left my hanky in the cloakroom,' or 'I've never told Miss Potts what my mum said I was to tell Miss Potts so can I go to tell Miss Potts now?' The incidental hazards of school life such as fire drill, lost property seekers and horrible little girls who had got all their sums right in the next classroom and had to be praised (through clenched teeth) added to one's difficulties when one had just embarked on a description of how to make a fishing hook from a whale-bone. Teachers everywhere, however, learn to take this sort of thing in their stride, and the real testing time came when one decided to 'make the model' and sent to the infants' department for their largest sand tray.

To get a really good winter scene of truly Arctic proportions at least six blocks of cooking salt were required. Even so this only allowed for two igloos worth their salt (sorry), but one realized regretfully from the outset that one can't have a large Eskimo township in a sand tray. Scraping the salt on to an old newspaper was always the thrill of the proceedings, and everyone, including teacher, itched to have the exquisite pleasure of slicing scrunchily down the side of a virgin block and chopping up any small salt rocks which fell from the snow face across such headlines as 'Hitler Says Patience Exhausted.' As knives are dangerous for young children to use for long one could usually have quite a good go at salt-scraping oneself, kindly allowing the more tender fingers to tip the loose salt from the newspaper and to spread and pat it into position. Licked fingers led to many a trip to the drinking fountain in the afternoon.

Shaping the igloos from half a block of salt needed more than sculpting ability. Near-perfect behaviour for some hours before the operation was one of the pleasanter by-products of the project and the final choice of igloo-constructors depended on this. At last the scene was done. Dazzling white ice and snow supported the two igloos, several Plasticine Eskimos, matchbox sledges with a somewhat bowlegged team of huskies to draw them and a polar bear or two and some seals kindly loaned from someone's model zoo.

For the first week all was as correct as seven-year-olds could make it. The fact that the polar bears towered like icebergs over the igloos could not be helped and no one quibbled about a few scarlet Eskimos when the flesh-coloured Plasticine had run out. An admiring group constantly clustered about its own handiwork and had to be shooed to desks before lessons could begin.

And then the rot would set in. It usually started with the unbearable smugness of the children who had brought the model animals. They were infuriating to those who had no Arctic denizens to add to the scene.

'That seal, see? That big one? That's mine. Cost fourpence,' they would say importantly, bustling about the table with a proprietorial manner. The reaction was inevitable. Gradually other small figures, hopelessly incongruous, would be brought along, and the pleas would be heartrending. Sometimes one could stretch a point by tucking a cocker spaniel in among the huskies, but it is trying a teacher's conscience too far to introduce a basket of kittens or a leopard into an Eskimo scene.

'Put them just at the side, on the table,' one would say weakly, so that the glistening sand tray would be edged with a pathetic queue of outcast animals. Sometimes model lorries would be brought hopefully or farm tractors and these would join the fringe of displaced objects.

And then, one morning after playtime, one would come back to the classroom to find that infiltration had begun. Just on the edge of the crushed salt – now a little greyer than before – would be a striped tiger or a red tractor, and one knew that the days of the Eskimos were numbered. They could not possibly hold out against the press of invasion which threatened their glittering territory. Next

week, we decided swiftly, we would set about the Sahara
and an oasis or two.

And so the glory passed and for the last day or so of its
fading splendour the sand tray would be a mad jumble of
penguins, elephants, celluloid babies and someone's tip-up
dust lorry. At the time one felt slightly guilty about it, but
looking back I can see that we were only a little before our
time. After all, Sir Vivian Fuchs was very glad to have his
'Sno-cats' under similar conditions in the Antarctic and no
doubt it is just a question of time before lions and lorries,
milking cows and mail-vans jostle with the igloos around
the North Pole. I, for one, will feel no surprise.

Harvest Festival

A sheaf of corn sags drunkenly against the needlework cupboard. The children squat on the floor among the straw like so many contented hens. They are busy making small bunches of corn to decorate the pew ends of the church which stands next door, and their eyes are intent on their handiwork. It is peaceful.

Every year, at the vicar's invitation, they spend the Friday afternoon before Harvest Festival Sunday in decking certain parts of the church, and this privilege they guard jealously.

'Shall we take some flowers for the font?' asks Anne, eyeing a fine pot of dahlias on my desk.

This innocent question creates a flurry among the straw. Hubbub breaks out.

'Us never does the font! The ladies always does the font!'

'That's right! Just the pew ends, vicar said.'

'No, he didn't then! The bottom two steps us always does. The ladies does the top two. Why, don't you remember how we done it with apples and marrows last year?'

'Me and Eric done it, Miss. Apple, bunchercorn, marrow; apple, bunchercorn, marrow . . . all round, didn't us?'

The point is settled. Pew ends and the bottom two steps of the font are in our safe-keeping, and peace reigns again.

'Make the bunches roughly the same size,' I suggest. 'Somewhere about thirty stalks, I should think.'

They lower their heads and their lips move as if in prayer.

'Twenny-two, twenny-three, twenny-four . . .' they murmur, brows furrowed. The line of completed bunches on the side bench by the wall grows longer and longer, and I call a halt.

'Sixteen pews on one side and fourteen on the other,' I announce. 'We need two bunches for each pew, so how many bunches shall be want altogether?'

There is a bemused silence. We can hear the vicar's lawn mower in the distance. At last John says he reckons us might need fifty or sixty, maybe. No one else has any other suggestion on this matter, and I put

$$16 + 14 = 30 \text{ pew heads}$$
$$30 \times 2 = 60 \text{ bunches}$$

on the blackboard. The side bench holds more than this number, so we tie up the rest of the sheaf with its hairy binder twine, collect our bottles of milk, and have a short interval for refreshment.

As they suck solemnly the children swivel their eyes round to the splendour of their achievement . . . sixty-odd bunches of corn, each tied neatly with the yarn that the smaller children use to knit, for their mothers, rhomboid dish-cloths; a wastepaper basket filled with polished apples; and a monster bunch of scrubbed carrots.

When the last milk bottle has clattered into the crate we go to the school door, bearing our gifts with us. Ann and Jane lead the way at a seemly pace, carrying the wastepaper basket between them. Behind them straggles the rest of the school, wisps of corn drifting from clutching hands to join the yellow elm leaves that flutter on the path between the school and the church. I struggle along in the rear, trying to find the best way to carry the slippery remains of the sheaf of corn. It pricks cruelly, and I dump it thankfully in the church porch for the other decorators to handle.

The door is heavy and opens with an ecclesiastical creak. The cold church smell, compounded of hymn books, mildew and brass polish, greets us, and the children tiptoe in with a subdued air. Four boys and four girls are dispatched to one end to attend to the font steps. The rest of them wrestle with their bunches of corn and the pew heads, lashing them securely with the lengths of knitting yarn which I snip with the big cutting-out scissors.

Above us, from the wall, look down the marble busts of the long-dead. Chill and aloof they wait, their sightless eyes gazing down at the perspiring children who are so zestfully enlivening their cold temple with the cheerful fruits of the warm earth. At last all is finished, and we go to see the final touches put to the font steps.

John is crouching there with an enormous apple in his cupped hands. He looks up, squirrel-like, as we approach.

'Us've done it, apple, bunchercorn, carrot ... apple, bunchercorn, carrot, this year,' he says. His voice is lowered to a hoarse whisper, in deference to the dead, but it pulses with a child's excitement.

He puts the last apple in place. We stand back and survey it with our heads on one side. There is no doubt about it. It looks absolutely splendid.

School Dinner for Forty

It's nearly dinner-time, children, so put away your readers and let me see who is ready to wash hands. Michael, *every day*, at the same time, you tell me your hands don't need washing, and I am beginning to get a little tired of hearing it. Everyone's hands need washing before every meal.

Who can tell me why?

That's right, Julia. To wash away the germs and dirt.

Your daddy bombed them, Richard? What do you mean?

The germs? Oh, *Germans*!

Yes, well, that's all behind us now, dear, and let us hope that none of you will be called upon to bomb anyone.

You'd *like* to, Richard? And you, Pat, and you, John, and you, Michael?

Good heavens!

Well, this won't get our hands washed, so let me see a nice quiet class.

The next boy who makes a noise like an aeroplane when I've asked for a quiet class will get a sharp slap for disobedience.

Hands on heads, shoulders, heads! The *fuss*!

All stand. Anna and Reggie can be leaders. Lead to the cloakroom door and wait there quietly.

I *hope* I can't hear a noise like an aeroplane, Michael!

First six, lead in to the wash-basins and don't dawdle. There are thirty-four more children to wash before twelve o'clock. The rest of you stand nicely. Don't push at the back there.

Children, it's no use telling me there's hardly any soap! There's a world shortage of soap and you must just make do with what is there.

Rinse your hands, dears, before you wipe them on the towel, then all the germs will go away with the water. No, Elizabeth, of course you can't see them. They're microscopic.

Very small then.

Next six. You people with clean hands can wait at the dinner-room door.

As you see children come out of the wash-basins, you others go in and take their places.

Heavens, here's the next class! Hurry up in there, children; you last few squash in together or we shall be late.

All ready? Now let me see a lovely straight line. Stomachs in, heads up! Wouldn't it be nice if our table were the quietest of all?

Lead in, dears. Don't push, children. Have the sense, Michael, to sit on an empty chair, not one already occupied.

All settled now? Hands in laps, and don't fidget with your knives and forks. Let's see if we can be the best table. I can see some lovely straight backs.

That's better.

Remember not to tilt your plates today as you carry them. I think it's stew.

What a horrid face, Jane! Thousands of poor children would be only too glad to have a *lovely* plate of stew for dinner.

All very quiet for grace. Close your eyes.

Shall I serve this container, Miss Judd?

Swede, I see. It always beats me how people continue to consider this stuff edible. Nice colour of course.

Pass along to me, dear, when Miss Judd has served you with stew, then go on to Miss Green, who will give you potato.

What, Pat, you *don't like swede?*

But look how pretty it is, and so nourishing! I shall put just a very little on your plate. Try and eat some of it, dear.

Come along, Jane, you've missed me.

Don't like swede?

Rubbish, dear, just a very little –!

Never mind about what you like and what you don't like, John Todd, eat this tiny little helping!

We don't want any tears, Elsie, there's hardly a mouthful there.

Next child, just a very little, dear!

Try to eat just a mouthful, Reggie.

You'll soon get used to the taste, Anna.

Any more for this lovely swede? Who would like a second helping? No one wants a second helping of this delicious swede?

My goodness, the teachers will have a lovely lot left for their dinners!

I like those people who have nice clean plates. Some very silly people have left good fat on the sides of their plates, I see. They won't grow big and strong if they don't eat every bit of it all up.

Good boy, Richard!

Pass your plates to the head of the table. Not so much noise, children, and don't *throw* your knives and forks on to the plates! Put them quietly side by side as I've shown you many, many times.

All sitting ready for pudding. I believe it's something you all like today. Jam tart with custard.

Hush! Hush! What pandemonium! If there's that fuss I shall ask Miss Judd to serve this table last!

Very well, Michael, as you don't seem to like jam tart you'd better go back to the classroom.

What do you mean, you do like it?

You're certainly not behaving as though you want to be served with some. That's better, and don't mutter under your breath!

Lead along, girls, for your pudding. Go to Miss Green for custard.

Don't tilt your plates, children! There now! Your poor distracted mothers! How will they ever get your clothes clean?

Now boys, and be careful!

Much better, boys. What is it now, Michael? You've got

a corner bit with no jam? Well, all I can say is it's rough justice!

Spoon and fork straight when you've finished, dears.

There's a lovely quiet table. Hands up if you want any more.

Miss Judd says this table may go first as we are all sitting so beautifully. Isn't that lovely?

Quietly lead out to play, and let's have no injured people trooping in while the teachers are having their dinner.

Play *gently*, all of you.

Thank you, Miss Judd, is this mine? No, no swede, thank you. I'd just as soon eat washing-soap!

Michaelmas Fair

'And it was *free*, Miss! The man gave it to me for nothing Miss,' persisted Patrick, holding up a jam jar with a lone goldfish swirling about in its cramped confines. Patrick was the most vociferous, this morning, among the scrum that habitually mills around my desk before prayers start. The other children, bearing less exotic burdens, such as bunches of dahlias for the classroom, squashed, purpling bags of blackberries, and polished apples for their elevenses, were full of admiration for Patrick's treasure.

'What you win it on? Them darts ... or rolling them balls into holes?'

'Ern's dad won him two goldfish, Miss, down the fair. Bigger'n yourn, Patrick.'

'They's got a great huge tank down behind the table. They catches 'em up in a net when you wins one.'

The cause of this feverish excitement was a modest Michaelmas fair, which puts up on our village green for a few nights on its way from the county town to the next one of importance. Our usual evening noises – the cawing of homing rooks, the jerky pealing of church bells as the ringers practise a particularly tricky measure and the crackling of autumn bonfires – had been drowned these last two nights by the braying of the roundabout's organ.

'I bet,' went on Patrick, unswervingly, 'I bet a fish like that'd cost two or three shillings in a shop. Fancy giving it away!'

'You gave the man sixpence, I expect,' I pointed out.

'Oh, my dad give him a lot of sixpences . . . one for each turn, but that was only for the balls,' explained Patrick. 'Of course, you has to pay for the balls . . .'

Finally, I drove them to their desks and opened the piano.

It was half an hour later that Ernest entered, opening the Gothic door with a thrust of his elbow. His eyes were red and he bore in each hand a jam jar containing a goldfish.

'Two!' gasped Patrick, with reverence. 'Good old Ern!'

The latecomer approached my desk and put his charges down carefully. Two wet rings appeared, hazardously near an imposing document headed 'Staff Returns'. I removed it hastily to the safety of a drawer.

'Sorry I'm late, Miss, but I had to clear up a lot of water for my mum, and she says would you keep my goldfish here as she hasn't got no room at home and they'll have to be thrown out else.'

There was a shakiness and gulping about this speech that told of much recent suffering, and I forbore to add the charge of unpunctuality to the sorrows that Ernest already supported.

'That's very good of you, Ernest,' I assured him. 'You can find the glass tank in the cupboard and get it ready.' Sniffing slightly, but brighter of eye, Ernest departed.

'You wouldn't like to put yours in as well?' I asked Patrick, moved with compassion for his cramped friend. 'There isn't much room in that jam jar.'

'The next door lady's got a bowl for him,' said Patrick swiftly. 'I'll put him in at dinner-time.' The glance he shot at me summed me up as a hardened fish-stealer. At twelve o'clock he was the first through the school gate, his jar in a grip of steel.

For three days Ernest's fish had the tank to themselves, disporting themselves gracefully and becoming grossly over-fed with ants' eggs, biscuit crumbs and an occasional splinter of toffee, cracked off the lump by the tooth of some particularly solicitous child. It was on the fourth day that Patrick appeared again with his solitary goldfish. It was now in an over-filled bowl, which slopped generously down his jacket. His demeanour was downcast and in his free hand was a note for me. It said:

> Please would you keep this fish at school as it is giving a lot of trouble and oblige,
>
> J. East.

'He'll certainly be much happier with the others,' I said to the silent Patrick. With head downbent he was picking furiously at a rough edge on my desk.

'And you'll see him every day,' I went on hopefully.

Patrick flung his head up suddenly. 'That ol' cat!' he burst out.

For one horrified moment I thought he was speaking of his mother, but I was soon enlightened.

'That wicked ol' cat! He put his paw in and sort of scooped Fred out. On the piano he was, and I went to hit him, and the bowl fell over, and poor Fred flopped down the back of the piano and all the water went in the top, and my mother let off awful and said I was to bring Fred to the tank here . . .' He paused to take a long, shuddering breath.

'Well, never mind,' I said soothingly, 'he'll be quite safe at school.'

'But that wasn't all my mum said,' cried Patrick, shaken to the roots by adult treachery. 'She said that Fred had cost my dad best part of ten shillings at the fair. And he never! The man *give* him to me, Miss. Fred was *free*!'

Damage by Conkers

'I've a note here,' I say, 'from Mr Henry.'

Nineteen of the twenty children clatter their pencils thankfully into the grooves of their desks. Abraham, the gipsy, remains with his head bowed. He is concentrating on some treasure hidden on his knees.

'Conkers,' I say emphatically, 'should be on the side.'

He remains engrossed.

'Or,' I say very loudly, 'they go in the stove.'

Without looking at me, Abraham shuffles nonchalantly across to the long desk which stands at the side of the classroom. A fine string of conkers dangles from his brown, bony hand. This ancient desk once served the grandparents of this class, six of them sitting in a row in sailor suits and zephyr pinafores; but now it is used for wet paintings, elevenses, jars of sticklebacks, and in September, for long tassels of horse-chestnuts.

Abraham manages to knock these with an adroit knee and set them swinging before returning to his place beside Patrick. Patrick, who is a meek seven-year-old with a pleasing gap in his front teeth, watches all Abraham's moves with admiring eyes.

'Mr Henry says that the skylight in his dairy roof was broken yesterday by a flint. He saw several of you throwing stones at his horse-chestnut tree. Well?'

Silence. Something suspiciously like a mouse rustles in the handwork cupboard.

'Who were the children collecting conkers?'

Two wavering hands creep aloft.

'Anyone else?'

Another one goes up reluctantly.

Ernest, whose hand went up first, here bursts out indignantly. 'Us wasn't the only ones. There was two others, wasn't there, Tom?'

Tom, arm aloft, nods virtuously. His eyes are fixed on Patrick, who is fidgeting uncomfortably. Beside him, Abraham studies his black fingernails as though he had just found them.

'We'll waste no more time now. Get on with your sums, and I expect the person who broke the skylight to tell me before the end of the morning.'

Abraham arrives first at my desk with his grubby arithmetic book. In the overpowering aroma of raw onion that emanates from his black corduroy jacket I put brisk blue crosses by his efforts.

He leans nearer, his face sparkling. 'I done it,' he says softly. He looks triumphant.

'Then you will explain to Mr Henry at dinner-time.'

The children mouth at each other behind their hands. Their eyes roll at Abraham as he swaggers back to his place. Patrick suddenly turns pink and whispers something to Abraham. Abraham rounds on him fiercely, one elbow raised.

'You shut up. You knows what you promised,' he hisses.

'Well, you shan't then,' bursts out Patrick, tears springing, and before our horrified eyes he rushes to the side desk, snatches the longest and glossiest string of conkers and thrusts them passionately inside his jacket.

'I done it!' he shouts defiantly at the class. 'He never!'

Abraham and Patrick now face each other like fighting cocks. Their hair bristles and their hands clench.

'Come here,' I command, 'both of you. Patrick, what is all this?'

'I was coming to tell you playtime,' he gulps. 'I done in the window, and Abraham was there too, and he said he'd take the wigging if old Henry come out, if I'd give up my conkers to him. But he never – come out, I mean – and I run home. And I'd sooner face old Henry meself than give him my conkers!'

He glares at Abraham, still clutching his bulging jacket.

I assume the mantle of Solomon, and address the tearful Patrick first.

'You should have owned up at once, and saved us all a mint of trouble. Go and apologize to Mr Henry at once.'

He departs – conkers, tears and all – and I turn to Abraham. He stares at me boldly, with black eyes a thousand years old in wicked wisdom. Solomon's mantle slips a little askew.

'Abraham,' I begin hopelessly, 'you surely know the difference between right and wrong . . .'

Conkers and Gingernuts

The first inkling I had of the whole sorry business was the arrival of a grubby note from David's mother. It was written, I suspect, on a page torn from the rent book, and in indelible pencil, for here and there blossomed smudged violet letters where the writer had licked the point. It said:

Dear Miss,
Am not one to complane as you know but have had terrible crying night with David something about his conkers but wont say. Could you look into it and oblige.

      Yours truly,

                         Annie Mobbs

David looked utterly weary as he handed over this missive. His eyes were leaden, the lids swollen. It was obvious that he was fit for nothing this morning but half a pint of hot milk and eight hours' sleep in a quiet room, with the curtains drawn. Our exchanges were brief but to the point.

'Who has taken your conkers?'

'Fred Bates.'

'Did he make you hand them over?'

'Not exactly . . . I sort of sold 'em.'

'Sold them! Who else is in this?'

'Pretty near all us boys.'

'Good gracious! And when does this business take place?'

'Playtimes . . . up the back,' replied the child, stumbling back to his desk. His head went down on to his arms, and he lay very still. I left him undisturbed while I digested the information.

Fred Bates is a lumpish, cheerful boy, whose mother keeps a little shop in the village and allows her son a generous part of her stock. I should have thought him too lazy to trouble to extort anything from his fellows, but evidently conkers were his downfall and he was prepared to go to criminal lengths to feed this unsuspected passion.

'Up the back' designates a murky, odorous corner of our playground bounded by a coalshed and the coke pile. Overhanging this spot is a rank and ageing elder tree, whose criss-cross bark is powdered with green rime. In the summer its white flowers float eerily in this underwater light, but now the purple berries hang heavily, and the ground beneath is stained with the trampled fruit. The children much prefer to crouch in this gloomy spot among the coke and beetles than to play in the open sunlight. I decided to explore the shady activities, 'up the back', at playtime.

As the children worked, I surveyed the long desk at the side of the room. The usual everyday things were there: lunch bags, two half-eaten toffee bars, their mutilated ends decently shrouded in paper, a curious snarl of metal that looked to me like part of a bicycle lamp and – a topical feature – strings of glossy conkers, some coiled, some dangling. At the far end were a few stout canvas bags, used for marbles at another season, but now storing the conkers of the connoisseurs, those who collected only a few perfect specimens and scorned to thread them commonly on strings. I wandered nearer, and saw, on the floor, between the desk and the wall, a knobbly pillowcase of striped ticking and, even more incriminating, a paper cylinder lodged on top of it. It was a half-pound packet of biscuits, bearing the words 'Finest Gingernuts'. I looked at Fred Bates, but that gentleman was industriously stabbing his desk with his nib and counting 'Twenny-five, twenny-six, twenny-seven . . .' as he struggled with his sums. I decided to postpone our encounter.

At playtime I threaded my way through the noisy children to the coke pile, and peered over the top. There in the gloom sat most of the boys from my class, their conkers at their feet. Fred Bates's great pillowcase gaped open to show, coil upon coil, like some brown, loathsome snake, his mammoth collection of conkers. In his hand was the packet of gingernuts. I retreated a pace and listened unseen.

'Come on, Fred. I've give you twenty, that's two nuts!'

'I don't know as I'm paying one gingernut for ten conkers today. My mum'll be finding out if I has to take too many. I'll give you one for twenny!'

'Dirty trick!' said an indignant voice. 'Don't you give 'em to him, John!'

'Tell you what,' said Fred hastily, anxious to keep his customers, 'I'll give you three for your whole string!'

'I'm not parting with me string!' said the first voice stoutly. 'That's what you done to poor old Dave, just because he was hungry yesterday. I've brought you twenny odd 'uns, ain't I? Well, then, you give us the right number of gingers!'

There were sounds of a skirmish, and I walked round the coke pile. We surveyed each other in silence for some time. At last I said, 'Go and stand by my desk.'

A sad little procession, swinging conkers and bolting half-masticated gingernuts, trailed across the playground, watched by their silent playfellows. In the rear, bent beneath the weight of his incriminating evidence, staggered the chief malefactor. As he approached the door, a shiny conker, as seductive as the apple offered to Adam, rolled towards him, dropped by one of his victims. With a savage stamp he crushed it to a pulp, and, clanging across the iron door scraper, entered to face his judgment.

Gunpowder, Treason and Plot

For weeks the children had been building the bonfire on a piece of waste ground, known in the village as 'the old pond'. Here, once, the little boys had waded out for frogspawn, ducks had floated and the cart horses, majestically slow, had stirred the mud with their great feet, as they were brought to be watered. Thirty years ago drainage pipes had been laid through the village, and the pond has become a scrubby patch of land, used as a playground by the children whose own gardens are crammed so tightly with cabbages, onions and cauliflowers (with, perhaps, a grudging strip of flowers as a sop to the mistress of the house), and there is no room in them for sons and daughters.

I had watched them, evening after evening, struggling along with all sorts of combustible material – discarded pea sticks, cardboard cartons, used straw, lino trimmings and, best of all, three old car tyres, presented by the local garage. Back and forth they went, as tireless as the rooks in the elms at nesting time, exhorting, encouraging and deriding each other as they laboured – their goal one brief evening of fire and glory.

At Mrs Mobbs's, the village shop, one corner had been given over to fireworks, and a brisk trade in rockets, catherine wheels and crackers had flourished all through

October. As the great day approached the curly bell on the shop door tinkled more often, as the children hopped down the step to see what was left on the dwindling pile. 'Golden rain', 'silver showers', 'witches cauldrons', 'magic fountains' – the names alone sent pleasurable shivers down their spines, while the acrid scent emanating from the blue touch papers was like incense in the nostrils of these young fire-worshippers.

Guy Fawkes' Day fell, obligingly, on a Friday, which meant that sundry burns, shocks, chills, hoarseness and other topical disabilities might presumably be dealt with by their parents during the weekend. In school, on Friday afternoon, excitement was at fever pitch, and, as an outlet for this pent-up energy, paper, scissors, paste and crayons were issued for making masks, which they could wear at the evening's celebrations.

They snipped and coloured busily. They measured raffia strands, for fastenings, as solemnly as tailors. They worked indefatigably until it was time to go home, and the results were agreeably fearsome. It was like facing a horde of trolls, I thought, surveying my enraptured class, for they had contrived terrible, grinning mouths, with teeth like tombstones and lolling tongues, pendulous noses, pig-like eyes, and even a pair of horns here and there. For a minute we lived in a nightmare world, grotesque and full of horror: then the masks were removed, seats creaked up, and the children stood to sing grace.

After the confusion it was quiet. I thought, as I watched them singing, how angelic they looked, with their pink, oval mouths, their clasped hands and their eyelashes resting on their downy cheeks. The thin tune quavered into silence . . . far away the church clock chimed the quarter, and the spell was broken. Off they clattered, more maddeningly noisy than before, clutching their masks to them.

'Get on, Ernest,' I say squashingly, 'and don't make trouble.'

He turns back to his book with a martyred sigh.

'Can anyone tell me an animal that goes to sleep for the winter?' I begin briskly.

'Cow?' suggests Ann.

'Pigs?' says Richard.

'If you listen,' I say with justifiable irritation, 'you can hear Mr Henry's pigs and cows at this moment; and here we are in the depths of winter. Think!'

There is a pained silence. While the class is cudgelling its brains the door bursts open, and Abraham and Patrick appear in a swirl of icy mist, sniffing happily.

'Where have you been?'

'Us 'as been snurling.'

'Do you mean snailing?'

'Yes, Miss.'

'Then say so. "Snailing".'

'Sneeling!' minces Abraham, in a tone of ghastly refinement.

I let it pass.

'Mr Henry gives us sixpence a 'undred. Pat and me started for him in the summer. We snurls his box edgings for him. They likes box, snurls does – don't they, Pat?' He nudges Patrick fiercely.

'Yes,' jerks out Patrick.

Abraham produces a threepenny bit as justification. Patrick follows suit with a mixed collection of damp coppers.

'Put them on my desk,' I direct, 'and hurry up with your nature work.'

They add their treasures to the drawing pins, beads, raffia needles and paper clips that jostle in the generous groove of the ink-stand, and clatter to their desks.

This refreshing interlude has brightened the class considerably, and 'dormice', 'squirrels' and 'hedgehogs' are put up on the blackboard. As I write – with the white end of the chalk – I ponder this snailing expedition. Something, somewhere, doesn't quite fit.

'Snakes!' shouts Richard, and now I know what has been puzzling me. Snails hibernate too.

I call Patrick and Abraham to my desk as the others work.

'Abraham,' I begin, 'does Mr Henry give you this money for keeping his box hedge free from snails? Or can you get the snails anywhere in his garden?'

'He only said us was to do the box,' he answers sullenly, looking at the floor.

'Did you find today's hundred in the box hedge?'

'Ain't no snurls there now,' he mutters.

'Where did you get them then?'

No answer from Abraham, but Patrick gulps and says, breathlessly, 'They's all stuck up in lumps, Miss, up the corner of the pigsty. And Abraham found whole nestses of 'em under a duck-board. They goes there, out of the box 'edge, winter time. Us gets 'em with a shovel.'

'And does Mr Henry know this? Or does he think you are spending a long time working along the box hedge?'

Abraham raises innocent eyes to the pitch-pine ceiling. 'Couldn't say,' he says airily. 'Not honest-like.'

'Not honest, Abraham,' I say wrathfully, 'is exactly right. You haven't lied directly to Mr Henry, and you didn't lie directly to me just now when you talked about snailing in the box hedge. But you have behaved deceitfully both times – and you know it!'

I pause for breath, and notice that I have an open-mouthed audience of eighteen children. Abraham remains unmoved, but Patrick twists a jacket button round and round unhappily.

'But old Henry –' he begins.

'Mr Henry, please, Patrick.'

'Well, 'e just said "sixpence a 'undred snurls" – din' 'e, Abe?'

'Mr Henry will probably go on paying you sixpence. The point is that he may not know that for six months of the year you are getting them by the shovelful, and in any case you are not working where he particularly asked you to.'

I flatter myself that Abraham is now beginning to look a trifle crestfallen.

'You understand,' I say sternly, pressing home the attack, 'that you are to tell Mr Henry where you are collecting the snails. Then it is up to him to decide whether he employs you or not. Now go and get on with your nature list.'

They retire, and I pick up the chalk, making sure that the working end will be white.

'Any more for the list?' I ask.

'Squirrels!' says John eagerly.

I point significantly to the board.

'Frogs!' says Peter. I write it up.

'Squirrels!' calls out some fathead.

'We've had more than enough squirrels,' I say shortly.

To my surprise, Abraham raises a polite, if murky, hand.

'What about snurls?' he coos. His eyes are round and innocent, his manner ingratiating. 'Ain't 'ad much about them this afternoon.'

Christmas Cards for Forty

Now this afternoon we're all going to make a lovely present to take home. People who fidget, Michael, will be standing outside the door and naturally there will be *no* lovely present for them.

Let me see if I can see two nice children to give out the paper. Don't hold your breath, dears, and don't push out your stomachs like that, Anna and Elizabeth.

Don't touch the paper till I tell you. We don't want dirty marks on our Christmas cards, do we?

Yes, Harold, they're going to be Christmas cards.

Don't touch!

There now! If you hadn't touched it, it wouldn't have fallen down and been trodden on! All put your hands behind your backs, and stop talking!

The fuss!

Everyone ready? Then listen carefully.

Fold your paper over like this and smooth it gently down the crease.

Richard, your hands! Look at that horrid black smear down your card. All show hands!

What on earth have you boys been doing?

Clearing out what drain?

Miss Judd told you to? I'm sure she told you to wash afterwards as well.

Well, anyway, you should have the sense to do so. Don't quibble! Great children of *five*, *six* some of you, and not enough common sense to wash before Art.

Very quickly run and wash.

The rest of you can sing a little song while we wait.

What shall it be? No, John, not that one your daddy taught you. Perhaps some other time. Let's have 'Bingo'.

Very nice. Here come the others. How wet you boys are!

Who threw water over who? Whom? Who?

Well, never mind. Let's get on or these cards won't be ready till *next* Christmas!

That'll do! That'll do! It wasn't as funny as all that.

All quiet!

Now let me see if the fold is by your left hand. *Left* hand, children. The side by the windows, then.

Good! Now don't turn them over or they'll open backwards.

On the front we're going to draw a big fat robin. You can copy mine from the blackboard.

Watch carefully. See how I use up all my space. His head nearly touches the top and his feet nearly touch the bottom.

Who can do a really beauti-ful robin? Use your brown crayon and begin.

Run along, Reggie.

All hold up robins. Some are very small. They look more like gnats.

Of course, Michael, yours would be different. Where are you going to put his legs?

A fat lot of good it will be to have them on the next page!

Right. Now shade a nice red patch on his breast like this.

Now inside in the middle we are going to write 'Happy Christmas' and underneath 'from' and then your own name.

I shall put 'from Mary' on the board but you will put 'from John', or 'Pat', or 'Michael', won't you, just *your own name*. Do you all understand? Hands up those who don't understand?

Carry on, then. Beautiful printing. While you are doing that I shall bring you each a piece of red wool to tie round your card in a lovely bow.

Richard, why have you put 'from Mary'? Is your name Mary?

Yes, I know it's on the board, but I explained all that.

Who else has been silly enough to put 'Mary'?

Nearly all of you! Now we shall just have to do them all over again! Another afternoon wasted, and we've got carols to learn, and the school concert tomorrow, and our class party to get ready, and Parents' Afternoon and all the reports to do before the end of the week!

Ah, well! Is that the bell? Lead out to play.

Richard and Joan, collect the Christmas cards and put them all in the wastepaper basket.

The Craftsman

'Seems a pity, really,' said Ernest reflectively, paintbrush poised above his Christmas card. 'All this work, just for one day.'

'You should've chosen a quick way to make 'em,' advised Patrick, beside him. He was experimenting with his first cut-out Christmas tree, a dashing affair, contrived from folded green paper. Ernest watched his neighbour's scissors making dramatic slashes in the paper, little triangles falling like confetti on to the desk, and he sighed enviously as Patrick opened out his successful tree.

'Done!' said Patrick smugly, and he applied a pink tongue to the gummed back of his tree. Ernest watched him place it carefully in the centre of his Christmas card. He thumped it with a grubby fist and leant back to admire the finished article.

'I shall cut out a bird, and stick him on just there!' He placed a dreadfully bitten fingernail in the corner. 'Then that's finished! Ten I wants altogether, counting my aunties.'

'Reckon I'll be lucky to get this one done today,' replied Ernest gloomily, bending to his task. 'Have to make some at home, I suppose, that's all. Threepence they wants at Mobbs's for cards! Think of that . . . *threepence!*'

'Ah! But they've got sparkle-stuff on 'em,' argued Patrick reasonably. 'That always makes 'em a bit pricey, sparkle-stuff do!' He counted nine pieces of green paper, stacked them neatly on top of each other, and started to fold them over. 'See, Ern? This way I'll get the lot cut out all at once. Bet I gets my ten done before your one! Old-fashioned, all that slow ol' painting,' he added scornfully.

Around them, the rest of the class drew and painted, folded and snipped. They had chosen their own means of making their Christmas cards, and it was interesting to see how their choice had varied. Most of the younger ones had chosen to decorate theirs with cut-outs of bright paper. Bulky, scarlet Father Christmases leant at alarming angles, awaiting white trimmings and black boots to their ensembles. Stocky reindeer tended to overflow the available space, leaving room for only midget sledges; and robins, balancing on the pin-point of their claws, like top-heavy ballerinas, were everywhere to be seen.

Most of the girls had preferred to use coloured crayons, and had taken infinite pains in drawing babies asleep, in cots that were so rickety that one would have thought them incapable of supporting the mammoth sacks that hung at their ends. Golliwogs, teddy bears, dolls, ships, trains and striped trumpets balanced at the mouths of the sacks, defying the laws of gravity in a remarkable manner.

Ernest's choice of pencil and paint brush was consistent with his habitual caution and patience. He had chosen to draw a church, set against an evening sky. Its windows were carefully criss-crossed into diamond panes. The door was grooved, and studded at equal distances with heavy pencil dots. The cross of St George floated from its crenellated tower . . . rather stiffly, to be sure, as if it had been well starched and was now aloft in a half-gale of unvarying velocity. All this minute work was largely covered when Ernest applied his paint, and had to be picked out afresh with the finest brush that he could find in the cupboard. Had he been alone his work would have given him unadulterated joy, but the sight of Patrick at his mass-production cast a shadow over his own slow-growing effort.

'When you thinks,' he repeated dejectedly, as he waited for his windows to dry, 'that it's all for one day!' It reminded me of Eeyore's sage remarks on the follies and fusses of birthdays . . . 'Here today, and gone tomorrow!'

'Never mind, Ernest,' I said, trying to cheer him, 'most preparations are just for one day. Getting ready is all part of the fun.' But such sententious nonsense clearly gave Ernest small comfort, and his mouth turned down glumly as he tested the church windows with a delicate fingertip. They had dried to such a fierce orange that one might be forgiven for imagining the entire contents of the building on fire, with pews, cassocks and congregation being done to a turn inside.

Doggedly, Ernest dipped his finest paint brush into the black puddle in his box, and, with his mouth puckered, began the slow, detailed work of picking out the submerged diamond panes. Beside him Patrick gave a sudden yelp of dismay. He gazed, in horror, from one hand to the other. In each he held the fringed fragments of half-Christmas trees.

'Blow!' said the mass-producer, scarlet in the face. 'I've been and cut through the blessed fold!'

With a smile of infinite satisfaction the craftsman beside him bent to his handiwork again.

Carols for Forty

I shall take you myself for singing this afternoon, children, as Miss Twigg is at home with a sore throat.

Can I go and open the piano?

Can I give out the carol books?

Can we sing the new carol Miss Twigg is learning us?

She's learning Miss Green's too, and we're trying to win 'em.

Remind me, all of you, to take yet another lesson on 'Learning-Winning' and 'Teaching-Beating' tomorrow morning. And I don't want bedlam either here or in the hall. I am looking for two conscientious and light-footed children who can lead this class at a rational pace from here to the hall door. John Todd, we'll see if you can take a little responsibility today. And Anna.

Miss Twigg always lets someone go first and open the piano.

Very well then. Pat, run ahead. Lead on, the rest of you. Don't gallop, John Todd! I might have guessed! Nor crawl, maddening boy! Just step it out briskly. Straight in, children, and stand in your usual places. For pity's sake, Pat, stop crashing the piano lid. You children seem to think that baby grands come down in every other shower.

Are we going to have carols?

Breathing exercises first, dear. All breathe in! Hold it! Out! *Much too much* noise on the 'Out'!

Miss Twigg says that's old-fashioned. She lets us do paper bags. We blow and blow at pretend bags, and then we *do* them, with a bang.

Very well. Blow! And again! Bigger still! Now pop! *One pop*, children, is more than sufficient. Miss Twigg's nerves must be in better shape than mine, I can see. All on the floor, sit. There is no need, Michael Jones, to roll about all over everyone else. Some of you boys make mayhem with a single movement.

Can we have our carols now?

Miss Twigg always lets us boys give out the books.

All hush! What is this squeaking that is going on?

It's our crêpe soles, Miss. Sideways on, Miss, to the floor, Miss.

Then sit still. I shall give the books out from here. Pass them along to the end, child. Brian Bates, don't hold us all up by peering inside each book.

I left a bit of silver paper in mine last week.

We seem to be six books short. Some of you must share. And that doesn't mean a wrenching match, John Todd.

You will be left with the nether half of that book if that's the way you handle it. We'll start with 'Good King Wenceslas' if it's in C. All listen quietly.

Miss Twigg don't play it like that. She always uses two hands.

That will do. Off you go, and anyone scooping 'Fu-oo-el', like a siren, stands by me. Stop a minute. Is someone singing bass?

It's Eric, Miss. He always honks like that.

Well, Eric dear, it isn't that you aren't *trying*, but your voice is rather strong, so sing rather more softly, will you?

Do let's have our new carol, Miss. Number ten.

One of those mid-European ones, I see; and unfortunately in five flats. I think it might be better to practise that a little longer with Miss Twigg.

Miss, there's someone hollering outside.

It's Miss Judd, Miss.

Open the door for her then. Perhaps Miss Judd would like to hear us sing a carol? There is just time for one more.

Please can it be our new one?

Would you like to hear it, Miss Judd? I think it would sound better unaccompanied. When I can see faces and not backs of heads, John Todd, and Michael Jones has stopped that silly giggling, and Brian Bates has pulled his carol book down from the front of his jersey, and Richard Robinson has quite finished looking at his tongue – I will give you the note.

That was lovely. While you were singing, Miss Judd gave me some good news for you. Miss Twigg is much better and will take your next singing lesson. Isn't that wonderful? For all of us.

Forty in the Wings

Miss Judd says we are on in ten minutes, and are we quite ready?

I hope so, dear. Stand still everyone! If you get so excited you will forget your words. Those wretched Holly Elves, stop sliding up and down in your stockinged feet. This is no time to get splinters in them. Any wobbly-winged fairies line up by my desk and I will put a final pin in you.

Miss, please Miss, you –

For the nineteenth time, Christmas Sprite, *go away*! You've done nothing but haunt me.

But, Miss, you've never done nothing about them bells what you said about.

What bells I said about? Stand still, fairy, or I shall never get these wings straight. Oh, the *bells*! Good heavens, boy, they should have been sewn on long ago. Fetch them quickly from the plasticine cupboard.

Do you know, Miss, I can't remember what I have to say.

Nor can I.

It's funny really, isn't it?

John Todd says he can't remember *nothing at all*. Not even the song part.

Don't panic so, children, it will all come back when you are on the stage. Simply remember to throw your voices right out to 'The Boyhood of Raleigh', and you will do very well.

John Todd says that stage ain't safe and we could easy go through.

'Isn't', not 'ain't', and if John Todd spreads such alarmist rumours I shall have to speak to him.

But, Miss, it does sort of squeak.

Simply the wood moving. You really are the most easily depressed set of fairies I've ever met. No more fuss now. All find a seat before I count three. Fairies, don't keep crashing into each other with those wings. I'm not made of safety pins.

Now when you are quite quiet – *quite quiet* I said, John Todd, fuss-fuss-fuss – I will open the door so that you can hear Miss Twigg's children singing carols.

For mercy's sake, that idiotic fairy in the front, take off those wellingtons! Nobody wants to see fairies galumphing about like a lot of Russians stamping the snow off their boots. Ready now?

Don't they sing lovely!

Very lovely. Lovelily. Beautifully, I mean. They've only two more carols to sing and then it's our play. Just make sure you've all the things you're supposed to have with you. Mother, where's your wooden spoon for mixing the pudding?

Them babies had it first for Miss Muffet.

Then rush like mad – *creep*, rather – to the babies' room and ask for it back. Hurry now, you are on first.

John Todd says he don't feel very well.

I'm not surprised at all. If I had been making the

hideous faces he has behind my back I shouldn't feel very well. All actors feel like this before the play starts. It's nothing to worry about.

I feel funny too.

My legs wobble.

It's my inside that feels the worst. It goes up and then down.

So does mine.

Never mind, never mind, no more complaints now. Let me look at you all and see if you are ready. Father Christmas, where's your beard?

I dunno.

What do you mean, 'You don't know'? You had it just now, didn't you? Where is it? Whatever made you take it off?

Too hot.

Too hot indeed, in the depths of winter too! Here's a pretty kettle of fish! Everyone search quickly. You as well, Father Christmas, lolling back there sucking your thumb while we slave all round you! The very idea! You are a thoroughly naughty little boy, Brian Bates, and this is the last time you are chosen to act, whether your aunt takes elocution classes or not.

Here it is, Miss, behind the radiator.

Pot black, of course, but you must lump it. Put it on at once and don't dare to take if off again.

Can't breathe.

Brian, understand this. Either you choose to wear that beard cheerfully, or Michael Jones puts on your costume this minute and is Father Christmas instead. Well?

Beard.

I should think so. Now we are all ready. I will open the door just a little. Not a sound!

I can see my mum.

So can I.

Here come Miss Twigg's children. Lead up on to the stage.

It won't really give way, will it, Miss?

Miss, I don't feel well.

Nor me.

Miss, them babies said they never had no wooden spoon off of us, so what had I better do instead of?

Brian Bates says he don't want to be Father Christmas, and he's not going to say his words.

Do we *have* to do this old play?

It's too late to turn back now, children. Fairies, point your toes, all smile! Right, boys, up with the curtain, and hand me the prompt book.

Sleigh Bells for the Village School

'Three o'clock, then,' whispers Miss Grove through the crack of the door between her infants' room and my own. I set my watch to the time shown by her massive wall clock, and with dark, conspiratorial looks we close the door and return to our excited classes.

The children are chattering like starlings. Term ends tomorrow, and at one side of the room glitters a Christmas tree. From its branches dangle small presents, wrapped in pink or blue paper, which swing slowly and seductively at every quiver of the floorboards.

'Do we have the tree after play, Miss?' queries an anxious voice.

'Eric says we have to keep the presents till Christmas Day,' says another.

'Silly! Us always undoes 'em in school!'

I assure them that the presents will be theirs before the end of the afternoon, that they can undo them the minute they get them, and then take them home. A wave of relief breaks over the class and they settle back in their desks in comparative silence.

'We'll put the writing on the back of our calendars,' I say, glancing at my watch. Five minutes to go yet before my own secret operations: I write 'To wish you a Happy Christmas. With love from' on the blackboard, and hear the clatter of pencils behind me.

'Don't copy it just yet,' I direct. 'Watch first.'

What I really want is silence, in both rooms, for the part I have to play in the lobby at three o'clock, and this needs careful timing.

'Can I wash my hands?' asks David suddenly. Confound the child, I think, nose to blackboard. I can't have him in the lobby at this stage!

'Rest your hand on your blotting paper,' I suggest. 'That will keep your work clean.' There is a general scuffling and ducking as this idea is taken up. Half a minute to go, says my watch. I saunter towards the lobby door.

'You can begin. I'm just going to fetch my scissors,' I say, thinking what an accomplished liar Christmas makes one.

The lobby is quiet and cold. The two classroom doors stand side by side, with 'Infants' painted on one in Gothic letters, and 'Juniors' on the other. The door-sill to the porch has been worn into a battered crescent by generations of sturdy boots, and under the door whistles a fearsome draught that catches one cruelly round the ankles.

I open the broom cupboard where my properties have been hidden, for the infants are to have their presents in a bulging sack, delivered by sleigh. Mine is the hand that drives the reindeer, rings the sleigh bells and drops the sack . . . and all in the matter of a minute, before uproar and mayhem break out in my own class.

I pick up the bells, two small silver ones fixed to a wooden bar, and tiptoe to the outer door. Here I shake the bells delicately. The sleigh is in the distance, but is approaching at a fine speed. The murmur which had come from behind each door is stilled as I shake more vigorously and creep nearer. Snow spurts from my runners, the fir trees flicker past and the reindeer spank ahead, heads tossing, silver plumes gushing from their scarlet nostrils into the bright air. It might have been as well to have had a conspirator with two coconut shells, I think . . . but then, with the snow as thick as this the hoofbeats would have been hopelessly muffled.

Close to the Gothic letters now I give one last ecstatic peal and then let the tinkling die gradually away, growing fainter and fainter, until I can hardly see the sleigh myself, nor the dark rows of fir trees, but only the line of wet mackintoshes hanging limply on their pegs.

I dump the sack by the door, throw the bells in the broom cupboard, grab the gardening scissors and return to my room. The children look strangely awed.

'Who was that, out the back?' asks John huskily.

'I've no idea. Why?'

'Us heard bells.'

'The church clock striking, I expect,' I answer.

'No, Miss,' persists Ann, 'more like little bells, Miss.'

At this moment a wild roar goes up from the next room, and Miss Grove appears in the doorway clasping the sack.

Around her is a milling mob and on her face a well-simulated look of stupefaction.

'Father Christmas must have called. Did you hear him?' she asks.

'Yes!' shouts my class. 'That was him! That was his sleigh bells we heard!'

'Put your calendars away,' I say, 'and we'll go and see what he's brought.' The infants vanish and there is a stampede back to desks in my class. Only David remains standing near me, lost in thought.

'If I'd gone to wash my hands just then, I reckon I'd have seen him,' he says, in a voice which is a blend of regret and perplexity.

'I don't know about that,' I answer. 'I didn't see him when I was out there.'

A long look passes between us. His mouth curves in a mysterious smile, as our gaze remains locked. Together, amid the hubbub, we share the unspoken, immortal secret of Christmas.

Snow on Their Boots

A shrivelling east wind had blown for a week, flattening the winter grass and withering the young wallflower plants. It had whipped cruelly under the school door, where the step had been worn away, hollowed by the scraping of children's boots for eighty years.

During the morning cold rain had lashed the latticed windows. Later sleet had appeared, and now, by half-past two, the snow came racing down, whirling blackly and madly as one looked up at it against the pallid sky, but drifting dreamily, like feathers, as it settled into the puddles in the playground. I decided to send the children home early. This announcement caused such pleasurable stir, such unbridled joy, that one might have thought that confinement in school was on a par with incarceration in the darkest dungeon, with periods of refined torture thrown in.

'Can you all get indoors?' I inquired, when the ecstasy had died down sufficiently for me to make myself heard. 'Is there anyone whose mother is out?'

'Mine's up the farm on Mondays ... scrubbing out,' said Patrick, 'but us keeps our key in a secret hiding-place, under a flower-pot by the back door, so I can get in all right.'

'Secret hiding-place!' scoffed his neighbour. ''Tisn't no secret if you tells us, is it, Miss?' Patrick flushed at this taunting.

'It don't matter if us all knows . . . not here in the village. It's for strangers like . . . those men as sells note-paper and that; and those old men walking to the workhouse.'

By this time Ernest's hand had gone up. His mother worked in the nearest town.

'I can go to my gran's, with my sister,' he said, his eye brightening. I knew the cottage well, and could imagine what a snug haven it would be to children on a bleak afternoon like this. The range would be shining like jet, and giving off a delicious smell of hot blacklead, its roaring fire reflected in the plates and covers on the dresser opposite; while, best of all, on the high mantelpiece would be standing the sweet tin, a souvenir of the coronation of King George V and Queen Mary, rattling with 'Winter Mixture', red and white striped clove balls, square paregoric lozenges and lovely, glutinous mint lumps.

They all trooped into the lobby, and there was a bustle of scarf-tying and glove-finding, and much grunting as wellington boots were tugged on. Away they all straggled, heads bent against the storm; all but one solitary figure, who was rooting about in the corner. It was Patrick.

'Can't find my boots,' he explained.

'See if they are by the stove,' I told him, pulling the pail out from under the sink. The most peculiar things got found here, but today there was nothing but a mammoth spider, which advanced in a menacing manner. I retreated to the schoolroom.

Patrick was running one finger in an aimless way up and down the piano keys. There were no wellingtons by the fireguard, and his feet were still shod in sandals from

which his grey socks protruded, the toes of his sandals
having been prudently cut off to allow for growth.

'Are they under your desk?' I persisted. He ambled off
and hung upside-down surveying his habitual place and its
environs, while I opened cupboards, peered behind the
piano and under my own desk. At last we sat down to
review the situation. We looked at each other, frowning.

'You can't have come to school in those sandals?'

'Can't've!' agreed Patrick.

'Someone must have gone home in yours by mistake.'

'Must've!' agreed Patrick. A heavy silence fell. The wall
clock ticked and a cinder tinkled into the ash pan. Outside,
a flurry of snow hissed against the window.

'Well, Patrick,' I said, at length. 'You can't go home like
that, and you can't walk in mine, so what's to be done?'

Patrick's eyes had assumed an intent look. I know it well. Thus does he look during multiplication-table practice, when, having had 'seven eights?' fired at him, he stands, with one leg curled round the other, awaiting inspiration. This time it came.

'In that old play-box,' he began slowly, 'there's a pair of boots what we used for the *Tin Soldier*. I can get into them.'

We hurried into the infants' room and threw up the heavy lid. Velvet capes, moulting feather boas, wooden swords, paper crowns, beads and fans jostled together; and there, beneath them all, were the boots ... an incredibly dandified pair of Russian boots with Louis heels. Very dashing they must have been a quarter of a century ago, but they presented a pathetic sight as they stood, side by side, with their tops drooping dejectedly.

Patrick sat on the floor, and, with much deliberation, forced his feet in. I hauled him up and we surveyed the effect. Patrick winced.

'Got my socks rucked up,' he said, and sat down again abruptly. Very slowly he began to edge them off. Outside, the snow fell faster.

'For pity's sake, Patrick,' I urged, 'hurry up. You'll never be home at this rate!' I straightened a torn lining, while he smoothed his socks. He put his feet in gingerly and stood up. Then he stamped happily, in the ridiculous things, to get his coat. I gazed anxiously out of the lobby window as he dressed.

'Tell your mother about losing your wellingtons,' I

began, when I became conscious of a certain tension in the air. Patrick was now fully muffled, and stood in the porch. His face wore its earlier look of concentration, mingled with some sheepishness.

'Come to think of it,' he said, in a still, small voice, 'I left 'em under the dresser at home, for my dad to put a puncture patch on.'

'*Patrick!*' I began forcefully, but, after one look at my face, he had prudently withdrawn, and was already battling his way across the playground, in his pantomime boots; preferring, no doubt, the storm that raged outside, to that which was so surely brewing up within.

Odour of Sanctity

There is nothing more welcome to a teacher, in the dark days of winter, than a bunch of flowers, particularly if it is her lot to work in an old-fashioned country school untouched by the hand of progress. Here the varnished pitch pine and chocolate brown paint so dear to our forebears makes a gloomy environment, and on a murky afternoon one has the feeling of teaching at the bottom of a treacle well.

It is true that we have some enlivening touches. A hyacinth bulb stands in a glass on the window-sill and has sent forth a seething mass of white worm-like roots. Constant lifting for inspection while teacher's back is turned, and too hasty replacement when she turns round again, have resulted in a large number of clubbed roots, so that progress in growth is slower than it should be. There are catkins too, at the stubby stage, and likely to remain so when one consider the numberless times the pot capsizes and that no one remembers to replace the water.

On top of the piano, in a pink saucer fast turning grey, stands a plant called Busy Lizzie, which bore many bright pink flowers in the summer, but has now had a relapse and appears to be hibernating. Now it is a known fact that Busy Lizzies thrive in the airless offices of the BBC, swarming cheerfully up little canes placed for their support by solicitous programme producers and burgeoning lustily in the windows high above Portland Place. This makes the melancholy plight of our own Busy Lizzie even more distressing, for blest as it is with a good blast of wholesome country air every time the door opens it seems ungrateful of it, to say the least, to dwindle as it does.

When, therefore, young Jimmy Gunner arrived recently bearing a fine bunch of yellow chrysanthemums he was greeted by me with cries of pleasure, although he was a little late.

'They're wonderful,' I said truthfully, sniffing the good-furniture-polish aroma. The stalks were very wet and Jimmy hastened to explain.

'My mum bought them yesterday at the market,' he said.

'Find a vase,' I answered, still entranced. There was an ugly rush to the cupboard by the door and within ten seconds a mob of panting children had deposited the contents on my desk. I suppose that our assortment of

vases is typical of most classroom collections. We have a
sturdy green bowl bought in the dear dead days beyond
recall for sixpence at Woolworths, a large monstrosity of
overlapping rhubarb-pink leaves weighing half a hundred-
weight and spoken of by the children as 'the ark pot', and
a bevy of paste-pots and honey jars of assorted shapes.

But the most useful vase, and the most hideous, is a
two-handled receptacle in deep blue dusted with gold. It
was won by a parent at the local fair and she had the good
sense to present it immediately to her young son. He
carried it to school the next morning as if it were the Holy
Grail. It has been dropped many times but is distressingly
durable.

The yellow chrysanthemums were arranged in this and
gave us much pleasure for over a week. Jimmy Gunner
drew my attention to his gift about three times a day and
basked in my flagging approbation. The morning after they
had been put into the school dustbin Jimmy was late again.
He lives at the farther end of the village and usually comes
with a group of others along the lane, although in fine
weather he can take a short cut through the churchyard.

'Anyone seen him?' I asked, pen poised above the register. There was no reply, but at that moment the door burst open and Jimmy entered bearing a particularly fine bunch of heather, white, pink and mauve. He handed me the bouquet, wet stalks first, with a beaming smile.

'This is all very fine, Jim,' I said, 'but you're late.'

The child looked pained at such ingratitude, but there was no time for further conversation. Assembly was about to begin and we were late.

Three days later Jimmy arrived with a magnificent armful of mop-head chrysanthemums. They were white and lustrous, every petal curling as crisply as a drake's tail. They must have cost a great deal of money. They were arranged beautifully and still had the florist's wire binding the stems.

Before I could question him, Jimmy said, 'A present from my Gran,' and escaped into the lobby bearing 'the ark pot'. The room had fallen remarkably silent, and I was conscious of nudges and looks being exchanged. As before, Jimmy had been the last to arrive, and a horrid suspicion blazed across my mind.

The child returned, dumped the pot on the floor, and began to unwind the wire from the stems. He sniffed villainously as he set to work, humming cheerfully between sniffs and quite oblivious of the ominous silence around him. My suspicions would have to be confirmed, but first things first, I thought.

'Use your handkerchief, Jim,' I said shortly.

Still sniffing, he jerked from his pocket a grey rag. At the same time there fluttered to the floor a small crumpled black-edged card. Jimmy's sniffs stopped abruptly as he saw it, and his face grew as pale as the blooms he held.

The game was up.

Winter Gloom

We were in the midst of the winter doldrums. This afternoon was one of those raw, murky ones that seem to go on for ever . . . typical of this most miserable of terms. Inside the classroom, four inadequate electric lights cast a pallid glow on the heads below. Outside, the sky was leaden, the grey lane empty, and the trees motionless. The vicar's tea-cloths, in his kitchen garden next door, hung stiffly, fringed with stumpy icicles along their lower hems.

We were having a nature lesson, no easy task at this time of year. Squirrels, bats, frogs and all the other hibernating animals had long ago been exhausted. Evergreen trees, domestic pets, weather charts and seasonal work on the farm had all yielded up their secrets. And we had fed the birds like mad.

There was not a flower in sight. Out in the lobby the dead Roman hyacinths lolled in their pots awaiting planting out. Only the hazel catkins cheered the classroom, and these I had fallen upon gratefully for our lesson this afternoon. Not that anyone wanted to work. The children were lazy, liverish and cantankerous – a legacy from the past few days of being cooped up – and I was not much better. The tortoise stove, as disgruntled as the rest of us, occasionally gave a hiccup and emitted a puff of sulphurous smoke where the lid was broken.

At ten to three coloured chalks and brown paper were given out. A hazel twig rested on each desk in a flurry of yellow pollen. Fingers had stealthily agitated the catkins to produce this heavy powdering.

'Look for the small red flowers,' I told them. This, of course, brought forth a flood of comment.

'Where?'

'No red flowers on mine, Miss.'

'Here – you got any on yourn?'

'Miss, we've sort of knocked ours off. Accidental.'

I became ferocious and demanded silence, and received aggrieved glances from all quarters of the classroom.

'I will draw a twig on the blackboard,' I told them coldly, 'and you can copy the female flowers from mine, if there are none on your twig.' I drew in silence, the chalk squeaked faintly, and then the first whisper began, sibilant and vibrating with suppressed joy.

'Snowing!'

''Tis too! Snowing!'

One, bolder than the rest, called politely, 'Miss, it's snowing!'

'It need make no difference to your work,' I told them, and bade them begin. Sighing, they picked up their chalks and drew wavering lines down the length of their papers.

Outside, the first few languorous feathers were soon followed by a flurry of faster ones, until the air was filled with mad whirlings and the snow hissed along the window-sills. Every now and again a child would stand up, the better to see this drama through the high, narrow windows, until he caught my stern eye, when he would subside again. The children's inertia had vanished, however, and they exchanged delighted glances. It was only when their gaze fell upon their work that their joy faded. Yellow male catkins, like fat caterpillars, and scarlet female ones as big as poppies flowered on every side. Another child stood up, catching its desk lid as it rose. There was a colossal bang, and cascades of chalk and a clattering Oxo tin fell to the floor.

'I was only looking at the snow
. . .' he began fearfully.

'I don't want to hear any more about the snow until this work is done,' I said wrathfully. There was a dejected silence and reproachful glances followed me as I walked up and down the aisles amid the two- and three-dimensional hazel twigs. Gradually the chalks were laid to rest and the dust blown from the masterpieces. At last, one chalk only moved, and that a white one. Patrick, tongue out, was stabbing away furiously at his picture, with a sound like a machine gun.

'What on earth . . .' I began.

Patrick raised misty blue eyes to mine.

'My catkins,' he said mildly, 'is out in a snowstorm.'

It is as well to know when one is beaten.

'You may all turn over,' I told the beaming class, 'and draw a snowy picture on the back.'

Outside the flakes whirled merrily, and inside the white chalks stuttered in joyful abandon. All was right with our world again.

Unstable Element

Ernest had paid a visit to Romney Marsh, and had returned much impressed.

'And all this grass, and little rivers and that . . . they was all under the sea once,' he assured me.

'Grass under the sea!' scoffed John derisively. 'Likely ennit!'

'It's quite true,' I told him, supporting Ernest, whose face was aflame with anger. John subsided.

'And this town Winchelsea,' resumed Ernest, 'it's a shame, really. Used to be right by the seaside, and now it's stuck up there, high and dry.'

'"Below the down, the stranded town. What may betide forlornly waits",' I quoted.

'Eh?' queried Ernest, startled. 'Yes, well . . . there it is, miles away now from the sea. Funny, really, the sea going away like that!'

'It's happening all the time,' I said, 'in a small way. Fetch the map of the British Isles, John, and we'll find Romney Marsh.'

John approached the marmalade-coloured cupboard, whose interior is a hopeless jumble of assorted objects, and, after some rummaging, produced a roll which, when untied, turned out to be 'The Disposition of the Tribes of Israel'. His second attempt brought forth 'Directions for Resuscitating Those Suffering from Electric Shock', noteworthy for the magnificent moustaches of the two chief characters. I found the map myself.

Ernest came out and scrutinized the lower right-hand corner closely. Triumphantly he slapped his ruler across Romney Marsh.

'There 'tis! See the miles of land there is ... all under the sea once!'

His classmates looked suitably impressed now that this evidence was before them.

'If the sea keeps all on going away from the land,' observed Patrick, 'England will get bigger.'

I explained that in some places just the opposite thing happened; and, remembering an incident of my own childhood, I gave a spirited account of the gradual encroachment of the sea on the Essex coast, with the dramatic climax of the falling of a cliff.

'And this movement is going on all the time,' I wound up. 'In some places the sea retreats, but in other places the sea is creeping slowly, but surely, inland.'

There was a heavy silence. 'Lor!' breathed Patrick, at length. 'Don't hardly seem safe. I mean, the sea's strong. Could get through anywhere, couldn't it?'

'Remember when we was paddling that time?' said a voice at the back. 'It knocked us clean over.'

'And sort of sucked us under too,' added another. The children surveyed the map with apprehension. I attempted to allay their fears.

'Of course, it's only a very little every year. Perhaps an inch or so . . .'

'That bit don't look too good!' said Ernest, coming out again, unasked, to put his ruler on the Wash. Fred Mobbs, who had drifted in with the milk crate some minutes before, now dumped it noisily and joined Ernest at the map.

'And just look at the way the sea's busted up here!' he said, indicating the Thames estuary.

'And look,' went on Ernest, with alarm, 'it's only got to eat through Essex, and Hurts, and Bucks, and this 'ere, to be at us!'

'What's more,' said Fred Mobbs slowly, his eyes riveted on the Bristol Channel, 'there's nothing to stop it coming the other side as well!'

I began to wish that I had never embarked on such a difficult subject as coastal erosion, or, now that I had been so foolhardy, that I had the support of a Fellow or two of the Royal Geographical Society to help me out of the mess. Time came to my aid. From the church tower floated three silvery quarters.

'I'll explain it all after play,' I said, with more confidence than I felt, and the floor boards shuddered as the children made their way out into the sunshine.

Ten minutes later, I discovered Ernest perched up on the school wall, demolishing an apple with noisy deliberation. His mien was thoughtful but rather more hopeful, and his gaze was fixed upon the comforting bulk of the Berkshire Downs.

'Come to think of it,' he said, pointing towards them with the tattered core, 'it'd take a tidy time to get through that lot, wouldn't it?'

Black Magic

The clock says seven minutes to twelve, and outside we can hear the splashing of twenty-odd infants in the cloakroom as they wash before school dinner.

My class, aged seven to nine, have just finished one of those rather dreary history stories about a little Saxon boy called (I think) Gumbroid. The children had not shared my ennui but had pored over the drawings . . . Fig. 1 Gumbroid's Bow and Arrow, Fig. 2 Gumbroid's Mother's Cooking Pot, Fig. 3 Gumbroid's Father's Picture of a Bull, and so on. Soon it would be our turn to wash, but meanwhile we have seven minutes to spare.

'Shall we sing?' I suggest.

'Oh, no!' comes the beseeching cry.

'Can anyone tell a story?'

A horrified silence greets this innocent suggestion.

'Mrs Robinson,' says a fat boy in the front row, 'lets us play a game.'

Mrs Robinson is their proper teacher. I am only in charge for a week, and Mrs Robinson's name is ever on their lips and her presence fresh and green in their hearts.

'Mrs Robinson,' they tell me, '*always* lets us sharpen our own pencils in the pencil sharpener!'

'Mrs Robinson *always* gives us our milk before playtime!'

'Mrs Robinson buys us sweets sometimes!' This is said with a hopeful, sidelong glance which is cruelly ignored. It is a good thing that I know Mrs Robinson personally and have the highest regard for her, otherwise my tolerance would be sorely tried. But the game idea sounds a good one.

'"Left and Right"?' I say brightly.

'We keep on having that,' says one child, so despondently that my heart is wrung.

'"Man and his Object"?' I suggest, remembering a game in great favour at this particular village school some years ago. But a new generation has gown up since then and the children look at me blankly.

'"Hunt the Thimble"?' I say, with enthusiasm.

'We used to play that in the babies' room,' says Ann crushingly. I apologize hastily, and an uncomfortable silence falls. Susan raises a hand.

'Can we play "Black Magic"?' she asks.

'Oh yes!' roars the class, enraptured. I signify my willing assent, and Susan bounces out to my table. She has clear brown eyes, the colour of a good medium sherry, and fine, straight untidy hair. We have grown very fond of each other during the week.

'Now, do you know what to do?' she asks me sternly. I confess my ignorance, and suggest that she chooses some-one else to help her.

'No. It must be you,' says Susan firmly.

'Mrs Robinson,' choruses the class, '*always* plays "Black

Magic" with Susan.' (I could hardly be blamed, I tell myself, if some ghastly anti-Mrs Robinson complex was firmly established by the end of the week.)

'I'll tell you,' says Susan kindly. She thrusts her face close to my right ear, and begins a long string of directions, given in a breathy whisper and involving a great many flash-backs of the 'I-forgot-to-tell-you' and 'Oh-and-before-that-you-should-have' type. Susan has once had a fringe, which is now at that awkward stage of growth when it escapes from its hair clip and sprays out in a fine fan across the child's brow. It tickles madly near my ear and I am almost distracted. At last, she stands back and looks at me doubtfully.

'Do you think you can do it?' Determined not to be outdone by the omnipotent Mrs Robinson, I say I can, but I am really hopelessly bogged down.

The class wriggles in anticipation, Susar corner and hides her eyes and I continue to stan. table.

'What is it?' hisses John.

'Is it the duster?' whispers Ann.

'Are you ready?' asks my confederate from the corner.

'No,' I say quickly. The fat boy has come out, lifted up a piece of pink blotting paper to show the class, and now looks questioningly at me.

'All right,' I say.

'*Ready!*' bellows the class. Susan, her face blotched with pink marks where she has pressed her hands, advances towards me.

'Go on!' she commands.

'What?' I ask blankly. Susan sighs. I am obviously a great disappointment to her. Mrs Robinson, I have no doubt, would have managed the whole thing beautifully.

The whispering and tickling is renewed. I gather that I am supposed to point to different objects and by some occult power Susan will know which one we have chosen.

I set to determinedly, armed with a ruler.

'Is it this?' I say, banging the timetable.

'No,' says Susan, confidently.

'This?' I say, thumping the nature chart.

'No,' smiles Susan.

'This?' I ask, hitting the blackboard squarely across Gumbroid's house, which bears an uncanny resemblance to my marmalade pot at home.

'No,' says Susan, her eyes shining.

'This, then?' I say, resting the ruler on the fat boy's head.

'Yes,' speaks Susan joyfully.

'*No!*' roars the class. Susan looks at me more in sorrow than in anger. I bow my head sadly.

'You never understood!' says Susan, heavy with reproach. 'After the *black* thing, it's the *real* thing. That's why it's called "Black Magic"!' I feel that I have let her down badly and am about to plead to be allowed another try when the headmaster puts his head round the door.

'It's gone twelve,' he says.

'We've been playing "Black Magic",' I explain.

He looks mystified but impressed.

'It's quite easy,' I tell him airily, 'when you know how!'

Stiff Test for Forty

This morning, children, we are really going to get down to work. Shut that window, dear. I can't hear myself speak with this howling gale.

What?
Not 'What'! 'I beg your pardon'!
Never heard what you said.
Shut the window, please. That's better. There seem to be a great many sleepy-heads this morning. All stretch! What time did you go to bed, Joan?
Dunno. About the middle of the telly.

The telly?

Vision, miss. Television, Miss. That's what she means, Miss.

That will do. You know that you *must* go to bed early. Now, no more wasted time. We are going to have a stiff test today. I shall ask you twenty questions –

Like on the wireless?

Not in the least like that. I might, for instance, ask you to write down the colour of a twopenny-halfpenny stamp.

Blue?

Sort of orangey-reddy-brown like?

Don't call out. Think. See who that is knocking at the door, Jimmy.

It's one of Miss Twigg's lot.

'One of Miss Twigg's children', please! Come in, dear.

Anyone lost this belt?

Look carefully, children. No, no one here. Now, back to this test. The stamp. Well?

Red?

Right. Of course, that's a very easy one. Shut that wretched door, Jimmy. We shall have the flowers over.

It won't shut.

Push it *hard*! Pick up those papers, Ann. I said, 'Ann', not a whole mob of you!

It's busted itself.

Let me see. A fat lot of work we shall get through at this rate! It's just one hindrance after another. We'll jam it shut with the duster until Mr Pratt can mend it. Sit down, everyone, and let's get down to work. Billy, give out the papers. Name on the top line, and I'll put the date on the blackboard. Where's the duster?

In the door!

Hush! I'll squeeze it up in this corner then. Number down to twenty.

The nib of my pencil's broke.

I haven't got no pencil.

Fuss, fuss! How many more of these maddening interruptions! Fetch one quickly from the pencil box, and let's get on.

I never heard how many you said number down to. The window kep' all on rattling.

Twenty! And why are you putting them down the *right* hand side, Brian Bates? I hope you are not adding mirror-writing to your other accomplishments. You don't want to be labelled 'Frustrated' on your record card, surely? Turn over.

The door's been and blown open.

Hold your papers while I shut it. Jimmy, help me to push this desk up against it. At least we'll have peace till we've finished our test. There! All ready? Let me hear no more interruptions. First question.

Jane says that was her belt what come in just now.

Jane, really! Is this true?

Yes, Miss. I just thought.

It's a pity you didn't think a little earlier. I refuse to go into all that now. We should be finishing this test by this time, not just starting it. What's that noise?

Fire bell! Coo– Good old fire drill!

Hooray! Fire drill! Get moving, boys!

Bet I win you down the stairs!

Bet you never then!

This is the last straw! *All stand still!* How on earth do you expect to get out of the classroom with the door smothered in desks? Let me come by. Now, without all this pandemonium, lead gently down the stairs, and *no pushing!*

Lucky you wasn't hollering out that first question at us, Miss. We might never have heard the fire bell!

The Visitor

In the empty schoolroom I am trying out the morning hymn on the fretwork-fronted piano when the confusion begins.

'Miss!' shouts Richard, crashing through the door, 'There's a dog come!' Close behind him stumbles a jostle of doubled-up children, embracing a mammoth foxhound.

''E followed us,' says Ernest hastily, after a look at my face. 'Din' 'e?' he appeals to his companions, but they are too busy caressing the hound to reply. It slobbers happily over their shoes and mooches in an amiable way among the desks, rather impeded by its limpet-like friends.

'Well, take him out again,' I say heartlessly.

'But, Miss,' protests Richard in a shocked voice. ''E's lost ... 'e's 'ungry! Why, he's etten all Ann's elevenses, and he fair golloped up a bit of bread Mrs Roberts chucked out for the birds!'

'He's just a poor, starving stray,' quavers Ernest, always a wallower in sentiment. 'No home, no food, and nobody don't want him.' The hound licks Ernest's knees with an enveloping tongue. Every fibre of his healthy five stones responds to this sympathetic treatment.

'Nonsense, Ernest!' I say, trying to heave the animal into the lobby. 'He's run away from the kennels, I expect.'

'They probably beats him cruel,' suggests Patrick, 'and that's why he's run off.' Hearing another kind voice the hound advances on Patrick puts its forepaws on his shoulders and snuffles at his face. Patrick, a puny child, topples quietly backwards like a ninepin.

'Oh, go and sit down,' I beg, hauling Patrick to his feet.

'He's a real loving dog, ain't he?' remarks Ernest in a besotted voice, as he moves off reluctantly to his desk. The hound follows him and pushes an exploratory muzzle into the inkwell.

'Now, where did you find him?' I ask.

'Up Four Acre, Miss. Over Dobbs's, Miss. Up the woods, Miss. In the playground, Miss,' comes the chorus.

'Well, never mind that then. Does anyone know if it belongs to anybody before I ring the kennels? I'd better do that before prayers.'

'Might be Springetts'. They walks hounds.'

'No, they never! Not since that row.'

'What row?'

'With them new people what come. You know, with them special chickens!'

'Special chickens? They's only Rhode Islandses!'

'That will do, children. You can give it a drink in the paint water bucket while I ring the kennels.'

I leave the animal to swamp the floor as it wolfs down a pint at each gulp. All the children have sidled from their desks and form an admiring circle round the bucket.

On my return all is deathly quiet. The children are clustered round the piano and make frantic signals to me to be quiet. Stretched out, the entire length of the instrument, is the hound, fast asleep, with its head pillowed comfortably on somebody's rolled-up jacket.

''E's just dropped off,' breathes Ernest, and I am not surprised to see that he is in his shirt sleeves.

'All go to your places and we'll sing our hymn,' I say, ignoring the exchange of scandalized and disgusted looks. I pull up the piano stool and play at arm's length over the recumbent hound. The children sing 'All things bright and beautiful, All creatures great and small,' with unwonted fervour, their eyes riveted on their unconscious friend.

It is while the last verse is in progress that the animal wakes, shakes his mammoth frame, causing a *vox humana* effect in the piano's vibrations, and ambles to the door. He sniffs the morning air and then, like a released arrow, streaks across the fields in the direction of the kennels.

A great gust of sighs goes up from all of us. But only mine is of relief.

Conflicting Evidence

There is the sound of a heavy body stumbling over the row of wellingtons in the lobby, and a muffled ejaculation. The children look up hopefully from their readers.

'I've mucked up the military formation a bit,' says Mr Roberts apologetically, coming round the door. (He farms next door to the school and is a frequent visitor.) 'I'll do 'em,' says John, hopping quickly out into the lobby before I can demur. The others look after the opportunist enviously.

Mr Roberts hangs his cap on the easel and wheels round, missing a jar of paste by inches. We all catch our breath. He is a large man: large in stature, voice and heart – and particularly in gesture. On one occasion he stepped back into the blackboard and easel, capsizing the lot, to the indescribable confusion of the room and the rapture of the class, who are always hoping for a repeat performance.

'I've come about my dog, Beauty,' he says. 'She's miss-ing.' The remark is addressed to me, but half a dozen children leap to their feet. 'Us saw him up Dunnett's, din' us, Eric?' 'Ah, he was up Dunnett's all right. Sees him coming to school s'morning.'

'Soppy! That's not Beauty. That's old Bates's dog.'

'I saw Beauty, sir. Up Netherend way she was, worrying the sheep.'

Andrew, always an alarmist, goes one better: 'I saw summink brown and furry, lying stretched out under the hedge up the top of the school road. Looked like Beauty,' his voice drops an octave, 'and dead, too.' If Andrew does not develop into a dramatist of the Grand Guignol school I shall be surprised. The children shift impatiently. 'Bit of old hearth-rug, more like,' says Ann, bringing us down to earth with a thud.

Taking all this conflicting evidence in his stride, Mr Roberts fastens on to one important point. 'When did you see this dog sheep-worrying?'

'Yesterday morning, sir.'

'That wasn't Beauty, then. She didn't slip off till last night.'

David now adds his mite: 'She comes down our place

evenings, when we're washing up the pots. Us gives her rabbit skins and she fair gollops 'em.'

'Well, I'd rather you didn't,' says Mr Roberts shortly. 'Did she come last night?'

'Yes, sir. Then went up Benn Wood.'

'Anyone seen her since?' Mr Roberts asks, sitting back heavily on to my desk. I shift the ink-stand back a foot.

Andrew tries again. 'There was a poor old dog tied under a gypsy cart . . .' he begins lugubriusly. 'Oh, you shut up, you old misery!' snaps David, voicing for once the feelings of us all. Andrew subsides, his face bearing the proud sorrow of all misunderstood artists.

As Mr Roberts starts to button his jacket, John returns from the lobby. 'Seen anything of Beauty, John?' Mr Roberts asks him.

'Beauty, sir?' He looks puzzled. 'I see her just this minute – out in the playground, sir.'

Snatching his cap from the easel, Mr Roberts rushes to the door. It crashes behind him, and there is the sound of a heavy body stumbling over wellingtons, a muffled ejaculation and ecstatic barking. With a sigh of ineffable patience John rises from his desk and, jaw set, makes once again for the lobby.

Rain on my Desk

'It always does that, wet days,' says the child with steel spectacles, patting the puddle on my desk appreciatively. I can't remember if he is David or John. This is only my second day as a 'Headmistress-on-supply'.

'Miss Pettit,' he continues, 'was always on about it!'

'Miss Pettit,' volunteers another boy, his lapels ablaze with badges, 'always shifted the desk over by the stove when it rained.'

'Once Miss Pettit had the register all of a sop. It come in during the night,' says the biggest girl. Her voice is hushed with respect, as if she speaks of Holy Writ.

The name of my predecessor rings in my ears every other minute, for Miss Pettit had guided this school of sixteen souls for many years, and any deviations of mine from her well-worn path are frowned upon by these young conservatives.

Steel spectacles and I heave the desk nearer the stove, out of the line of the drops which fall inexorably from the skylight. The floor is awash, and I notice how rotten the boards are becoming.

'Fetch the duster,' I direct, 'and mop the desk first.'

There is an ugly rush to the easel and a chubby infant emerges triumphantly, duster in fist.

'We must get someone to mend it,' I say. 'Who is there in the village?'

'My dad,' says the badges boy promptly.

'He never does the school windows,' protests Edward, who, at eleven, has reached that dizzy pinnacle of responsibility, head boy. 'Miss Pettit always sent for old Williams, Miss, down the forge, Miss. He done it twice last summer.'

The rain drips rather faster, as comment on old Williams's workmanship. I put the paint bucket to catch the drops.

'Take out your readers,' I say, 'while I write a note to Mr Williams. I shall be looking for a sensible child to take it.'

Silence falls. Backs are stiff, chests thrown out and books are scrutinized closely. Even the chubby infant, who is not yet five, pores over his scrapbook and gazes at an antique advertisement for Mazawattee tea with unnatural fervour. To escape from school for an enchanted ten minutes; to mingle with the grown-up world of driving cattle and flapping sheets . . . What joy that would be!

I look up when I finish writing. It is as though a spell lies upon the children. Eyelashes brush cheeks. Lips move as if in prayer, boots are set primly side by side.

'Edward!' I say, and he leaps forward. The spell is broken, and a sad little sigh goes up from the class as Edward slams the door behind him.

A wide crack runs across the weather-beaten desk-top. I pull out the top drawer and remove several wet books. One of them has handsome marbled edges, and the words 'Log Book' stamped in gilt on the leather cover.

While I am mopping out the drawer Edward returns with a grubby note. It says:

Will com this afternoon have done skylit three times recently and waste of time it is but will com.

Sign A. Williams

A particularly sharp burst of rain spatters on the skylight and the din in the bucket is intensified.

'Miss Pettit,' says Edward reprovingly, 'always put a bit of rag in the bottom to stop the noise.' I bow to Miss Pettit's shade and meekly reach for the duster.

'Not that!' shrieks Jane from the front desk. 'The floor cloth Miss Pettit always used! It's under the sink.'

She vanished into the lobby and I retire to my seat near the tortoise stove. I wonder to myself how many months Miss Pettit suffered from our present afflictions. It was to be hoped that it was a recent flaw in the school's fabric, and she had not endured this every wet day throughout her fifteen years of office.

Jane returns with the floor cloth and folds it neatly to fit the bottom of the bucket. The sonorous clangs change suddenly to muffled thuds. Relief floods the room and I idly open the log book.

The page is headed April, 1883. The ink had faded to fawn, and I read the first entry written in a clear square hand.

'Arithmetic lesson curtailed this morning as the Master and Four Boys were obliged to repair skylight which was letting through rain on to the Master's desk below, to the detriment of Furniture, Flooring, and Books . . . '

Thirty-one and a Donkey

'He's always called Junior,' explained his young American mother, 'but I guess you'd best put Duke down, for the record.' So I wrote 'Duke Schuster' in the register of the village school, and added '10.4.1946' in the column headed 'Date of Birth'.

He said goodbye to his mother with composure, and gave no sign of noticing the stares of his classmates. There he sat, tragic and aloof, his thin arms, like peeled willow wands, propped up on the desk. Peter, sitting beside him, looked him over soberly from his bleached crew-cut to his stubby American boots. At last he ventured a remark.

'I collect car numbers,' he said.

'Uh-huh!' replied Duke politely, without turning his head.

'And John, just behind you,' I said, a shade too brightly, 'collects tractors. He once saw seven in one day.' Duke gave a small, social smile, and I made one more attempt at breaking the ice before morning prayers.

'When I was a little girl we used to collect horses. You had to see thirty-one to finish the game, and if you saw a donkey you had to start all over again.'

The child's eyes kindled. 'Thirty-one, eh?' he repeated, with interest. 'In any set time, ma'am?'

'Oh no! I once took three weeks to get to twenty-nine, and then I saw a donkey, so that finished that game.'

'Sure, that was tough!' said Duke with real feeling, and, straightening his vivid shirt, he rose with his companions for the hymn.

The weeks went by. Marbles, skipping-ropes, balls and five-stones took their turn in the playground, while cowboys and spacemen jostled with mothers-and-fathers in cheerful confusion.

Duke did not join in any of these games. He did not appear to be unhappy: he was not bullied or molested in any way. Occasionally he would watch a particular game but always he returned to his chosen spot, hanging over the school wall, his pale legs dangling and his eyes fixed on the dusty lane. Sometimes he slid down, prised a piece of rough chalk from a secret crevice in the wall, and added a mark to a line of ticks wavering along the bottom. Then he would clamber back to resume his vigil.

'Why don't you ask Duke to play cowboys?' I suggested one day, coming upon a posse of them crouched behind a pile of coke.

'He likes his own game best,' explained one of them,

adding casually, 'He just don't want to play our things.'
He cocked two fingers, set up a machine-gun stutter, and
crunched madly away over the coke. There was no dislike
in his tone; simply indifference. It was quite plain that
there was no enmity on either side; and equally plain that
there was not a vestige of Anglo-American good will.

Some of the children went home at midday, including
Duke, while others had dinner at school and then ran
about in the playground. During one sultry dinner-hour,
the plant-man made his annual call at the schoolhouse. He
was a likeable rogue, in layers of waistcoats and pullovers
of many colours. His little cart, carpeted with velvety
pansies, double daisies and forget-me-nots, was drawn by
an ancient donkey that walked, sweetly and mincingly,
with unhurried steps.

As I was rubbing its plushy nose and choosing my
plants, the hubbub broke out. The children ran out from
the school gate, and away down the road calling frantically
to each other.

'He's just come out of his gate!'

'Well, git on and stop him, silly! We best lead him, I reckons!'

'Poor old Dook! Touch luck, eh?'

The plant-man was digging his wares out with a broken spoon and placing them carefully on an out-spread newspaper.

'That'll be five bob, lady; and every one a prize 'un,' he told me. His teeth were black and he reeked of onions. As I paid him, the children returned. In their midst, eyes tightly shut, was Duke. His slender arms were outstretched, supported by Peter and John, while all around him the children proffered agitated advice and encouragement.

'Keep 'em closed, Dook. You're all right, mate! It's moving off, look! Don't you open your eyes, Dook, till us says!'

They advanced raggedly to the school porch. I dumped my newspaper parcel by the gate and ran, full of awful forebodings, towards them. The clip-clop of the donkey's hooves faded away as the cart vanished round the bend of the lane, and a great sigh went up from the children.

'Safe now, Dook! He's gone!' They milled around him, rejoicing, grubby hands thumping his bright shirt as he blinked dazedly in the sunshine. Suddenly he broke away from them and ran across to his old haunt by the wall. The others swarmed after him excitedly, buzzing like bees after their queen.

He pointed to the chalk marks at the foot of the wall, and turned grinning from ear to ear.

'Thirty, ma'am,' he yelled back to me, 'and tooken me six weeks!'

Economy for Forty

Michael Jones! There is no need to screw up that perfectly good piece of gummed paper, wasteful child! It would do quite well for grass or leaves – or even a green butterfly, at a pinch. Which reminds me – Scissors down for five minutes!

'Oh, miss! Peter Patey's tooken mine!

I never!

He did – honest! They're sharper than his, that's why he went and –

All scissors on desks! Who is that wilful little person who is daring to chink them when I've said put them down?

Brian Bates!

No tales, please. Put your scissors on my desk, Brian. Is this your tuft of hair in them?

No.

Whose then?

Don't know nothing about it.

Brian, answer me truthfully.

Well – It's a bit off of Jane's plait. It was lying all across my ink-well, and it sort of went in, so I just nicked the inky bit off for her.

Naughty little boy! Stand by the board, and I'll sort this out at playtime. All heads this way. I have something serious to say to you.

Is the dentist coming?

No, no! But Miss Judd has had a very important letter from the office, asking everyone in this school – you as well, John Todd, and a good sharp slap will you get, my boy, if you go on fidgeting with your scissors – Where was I?

The letter.

Oh, yes. We are all to be as *careful as possible* with every single thing we use in school.

What like, say?

Paper, for instance. You heard me telling Michael not to waste that piece of sticky paper. It is very expensive.

But that inspector lady last week said we was never to have such tichy bits. Why, she give me a whole sheet of blue for my sky.

H'm, yes! I know. That was rather different, dear. Now, you understand? *No waste anywhere!* Not only paper, but pencils too. They all cost money and we shall be helping our country if we are really careful.

You went and chucked mine in the wastepaper basket. You said it was too short.

Then in that case it was. And I don't care for your tone, boy. Can you think of any other ways in which we can economize?

Can what, Miss?

Save money, then?

Bringing savings?

Yes, but I meant actual things. Paper and pencils we've mentioned. Anything else?

Dinners?

A very good point, Jane. Let us have no more nourishing

fat and health-giving greens left on the plate rims. After all, thousands of poor children in other countries –

My mum always says that!

And mine!

Quite right too. Any more ideas?

We could do without tests, and spellings and all that. It would save heaps of paper. And your marking pencil!

That's going a little too far, perhaps.

Couldn't we end school a lot earlier, and save coal?

Yes, well . . . I think all that is rather drastic. We don't want to impair the essential fabric of education. Can you think of anything else? Quickly now, and then we really must finish cutting out this spring frieze or it will be Christmas by the time we get it up. Well, Andrew?

When I was home with the mumps I listened to the wireless when it had lessons on. I remember it ever so well. It was something about some people what lived in some other country, or something.

The television learns you too, really.

'Teaches you', not 'learns you', child! The times you've been told!

Tell you what, Miss! I've just thought. If the telly and wireless learnt us at home we wouldn't need no schools at all!

We'd save all our books!

And paints, and clay, and sand trays!

And school dinners!

We could even do without teachers, couldn't we?

It seems a very sound idea, John. I will get Miss Judd to put it to the Director of Education. Meanwhile, we'll economize with our cutting out. All pick up scissors, and work twice as fast to make up for lost time. Brian Bates, back to your place now – and don't you dare to screw up those blue shreds after all I've said! They will make perfectly good forget-me-nots . . .

The Real Thing

The last drawing-pin has been thrust into the creaking partition, and the children stand back among a welter of paste-pots, brushes and coloured paper to admire their new spring frieze. It is of surprising beauty, blazing a trail right round the classroom, from the raffia cupboard to the tortoise stove.

It has taken many hours of tongue-writhing child labour to make, for everyone's efforts are there. Even Henry, who started school only last week, five and frightened, has added a magnificent hybrid to the garland of flowers; and his fat thumb still bears the ring made by his hard-working scissors.

Crocuses, snowdrops, daffodils, tulips and many exotic blooms as yet unknown to Messrs Sutton, Carter, Rayner and their illustrious colleagues riot along the walls, and as they billow gently, still damp from the paste brush, we glow with achievement.

'Clear up quickly,' I say, 'and I'll start reading your new book this afternoon.'

With squeaks of joy the children dash about the room, thrusting brushes into jam jars, squashing damp newspapers, which have covered the desks, into glorious glutinous balls, and grovelling on the floor for bright scraps of paper. Back and forth they dart to the wastepaper basket – artists every man-jack of them – with the beauty of their creation encircling them.

Amid the turmoil I thread my way to the bookshelf and take out *The Wind in the Willows*. I had planned to start it next term, but what more fitting occasion than this could be found for beginning such a spring song? Around me buzz the busy children, bumbling against my knees as they grope after stray fragments.

'Sorry, Miss. Never saw you there, Miss,' or ''Scuse me, Miss ... 'sunder your shoe.' They swish and swirl sibilantly about me, until I return to the safety of my desk.

'I'm ready!' I call, above the hubbub, and as they settle, with a last flurry, I look with pride at our spring-like classroom. For, as well as the new frieze, there is frogspawn a-glimmer in the glass tank, violets on the window-sill and some horse-chestnut twigs thrusting out downy hands from the nature table. An early red admiral butterfly has settled on *Hymns Ancient and Modern* on top of the piano,

and semaphores spasmodically with its bright wings. At
the back of the classroom is the weather chart, headed in
wobbly capitals 'SPRING TERM'
Each square represents a day,
and snowmen, umbrellas and kites
give some idea of the mixed
weather we have endured; but
four heartening suns in a row
beam, like yellow daisies, from
the last spaces.

At last peace reigns, and I
begin. Only little Henry, tired and
sticky after his handwork efforts, is
restless. He flings his arms across the desk and props his
chin upon them. From his mouth he blows bored, glassy
bubbles, his eyes fixed vacantly upon the window. I read
on steadily ... 'The Mole had been working very hard
all the morning, spring cleaning his little home ... ' but
after a page or two I am conscious that Henry's restlessness
is infectious. There is an occasional sigh, a scuffling, and I
realize suddenly that they are not really listening. Something, somewhere, distracts them.

Henry, at this moment, pops an enormous bubble with
pursed lips, clambers from his place and runs forward. His
face is desperate. 'Say,' he urges loudly, 'let's go out!'

There is a shocked silence. What madness is this? And will it make me fly right off the handle? An apprehensive shiver runs round the classroom. I look at the stunned children. 'Shall we?' I ask.

Their anxiety melts in a moment. 'Yes!' they roar rapturously, and tumble higgledy-piggledy into the lobby. Once out in the playground they skip for joy at this unexpected freedom. This is what had distracted them, back there in the classroom, the imperious, clear call of spring. Up above us the elm trees glow with rosy buds, and in their highest branches the squawking rooks squabble over stolen sticks. The air is warm, heady and honeyed with unseen flowers.

'Run as fast as you like across the meadow,' I tell the gambolling children, and as they tear off, legs twinkling, hair flying, I lean against the sunny school wall, sparking rainbows through my lashes, and pondering on the wisdom of young Henry, who, surrounded by the tokens of spring in the classroom, had realized that they were only substitutes for the real thing.

It was he, the babe among us, who had led his befuddled elders to reality when he had cut straight to the heart of the matter with those three words, 'Let's go out!'

Nature Walk for Forty

Miss Judd says we may all have a great treat today and go out for a lovely walk to see the trees. Yes, John, I dare say you have seen them, but this is rather different. We are going for a nature walk to learn the names of the trees, and to see if we can find any buds and leaves. Won't that be lovely?

When we're all sitting properly I shall choose two sensible children for leaders. What are you doing under the desk, Michael?

He's what, John?

Eating!

Bring it here, Michael. What a nasty, messy orange! Put in on a piece of paper on the cupboard and don't let it happen again. Eating indeed! I never heard of such a thing!

Well, now, let me see who looks bright and sensible. I can't say you do, Reggie. Close your mouth, dear, and breathe through your nose. Like this.

No, dear, *like this*.

All breathe in. Yes, well –!

Before we go we'll have handkerchief drill. Hold up hankies. Not many this morning, I'm afraid. Hands up those who have forgotten them. Anna, give out the paper ones.

Right, now let's try again. Breathe in. And out. In and out. Much better. Hankies away.

Pat and Elsie, come to the door. You shall be leaders today. Walk very nicely and stop when I tell you, otherwise the back children won't be able to keep up.

The rest of you come out quietly.

Quietly!

Go back again and sit down.

If there's that dreadful fuss again *we don't go* for this lovely walk!

Very quietly, creep out like mice.

Much better. Hold hands with your partner.

Lead on, Pat and Elsie, to the cloakrooms. If you have wellingtons put them on; it is rather wet in the road.

Can't you tie up laces yet, Peter? Yes, I know you can, John, and you, Pat, and you, Julia. Help him with his shoes, Julia.

Anyone else who wants help with laces?

Who is ready? Stand by the wall in a nice line, and don't push, Michael. Hurry up in there, you others, or we shan't get out today.

Who tied up Peter's shoes? Well, surely you could see he had them on the wrong feet? Change them over, Peter.

Whose wellington is this? No name, of course. Children, you must ask your mummies to put your names in your wellingtons.

You *what*, Richard?

You *told* your mummy she'd *got* to?

Then I don't blame her for not doing it? *Got to*, indeed!

I'm sure I didn't say anything of the sort. Ask your mummies if they would be kind enough to put your names in, that's what I said, Richard.

Everyone look! Eyes to the front! Eyes on this wellington!

Now, whose is it?

It must belong to someone!

Are you sure it's Reggie's? Where is he? Has he gone out there with only one wellington on? Peter, run and tell him to hurry and ask him if he's lost a wellington.

The rest of you stand nicely and listen to me.

We're going to walk down the school road and up the chestnut avenue. Leaders, wait at the gate until I tell you to lead on.

Come along. Reggie and Peter, hold hands at the end and don't straggle. Off you go, leaders.

Look where you are going, children, don't turn your heads round this way or you'll trip over.

There now, Pat, you should look in front.

What a beautiful sunny morning! Wait, leaders, *wait*

Leaders, you must listen, or we shall all be strung out for miles.

Now, this big tree is an oak tree. Do you know what grows on it later on? Yes, leaves of course. What else?

No, not apples, nor plums. Think again. That's right, Anna, acorns. Do you remember we made some little men with acorns and pins last autumn? Look again at the oak tree.

Right, lead on. Don't rush so, leaders, wait at the next lamppost. Hurry up, Reggie and Peter, keep up with the others.

Stop again, leaders, here is another tree. It had some pretty pink flowers on it a little while ago. Do you know its name?

No, not a rose. A rose has prickles.

An almond tree. It will have nuts in the autumn, won't that be lovely?

Oh, here comes the milkman and his horse. Don't touch it, Julia, it may not like children. Oh, he does, milkman? Good, may we give him a bunch of grass? Not all of you. We'll choose someone nice. Jane, would you like to feed him?

Of course he's not a mad horse, Michael. What on earth makes you say that? Because of the froth round his mouth? Don't be silly, that froth is only, well – froth.

That will do, then, Jane, wipe your hand, dear.

Jane, dear, not all down your new coat? Where's your hanky? Take mine. Say goodbye to the horse, children, but don't shout so. You will deafen it.

Lead on to the chestnut avenue. Look at these lovely sticky buds. I'll pick some for the classroom. Can you see the horseshoe marks on the stem. Don't all push. Stand in line and I will let you all see in turn. These beautiful twigs grew on the horse-chestnut tree.

Stand still, children! Listen!

Good heavens, the children are out at play already!

All turn! Reggie and Peter, you can be leaders. We shall have to hurry back and have our milk after play today.

Step out, children. Don't tread on the child's heels in front, Michael, it is most painful.

If we meet Miss Judd we shall be able to tell her we've seen an oak tree, an almond tree and a horse-chestnut tree, shan't we?

And I hope you'll all know which is which!

Wild Surmise

'Who knows why Patrick is away?'

Sixteen junior heads tilt up. Sixteen hands cease drawing tractors, misshapen girls skating, or the cat asleep, according to the age and sex.

'Never knew he wasn't here,' remarks James helpfully. He is looked at, and subsides.

'He was all right Friday. Come frogspawning. All us Batley lot went, didn't us?'

A chorus of assent as the class warms up.

'He never come to Sunday School though, Sunday.'

'Ah well, he's chapel.'

'That he's not! He sits in our pew regular, don't he, Jim?'

'His mum has been bad, Miss. Perhaps he's looking after her.'

'Well, she was banging her mat as I come along, and hollering across to old –'

'That'll do, that'll do. One of you can go into the infants' room and see if his little sister is here.'

An unnatural hush falls. The wind blows under the Gothic door and 'Pond Life in Early Spring' rustles from the wall to the floor. Even then there is no rush. Sixteen

faces assume expressions of fierce intelligence
and responsibility. The infant teacher keeps
a jar of boiled sweets.

'Ann.'

Smug in pink check and ringlets she
bounces triumphantly through the adjoining
door. The boys exchange disgusted looks
and shade in their tractors . . .

'She's not there neither,' says
Ann, returning with a delicious bulge in her cheek. The
boys look sourer than ever. These old girls! All hang
together!

'They do say there's flu up Netherend.'

'Ah, he got pretty wet too, spawning Friday, didn't he?'

'All up his legs. His mum carried on at him.'

'Now I come to think, we saw nurse's car up that way
Saturday morning, didn't us?'

'That was outside Bates's. My dad said Frank Bates was
cleaning out the carburettor for her, save her taking it to
the garridge, because he's got them two motor bikes to
mend what crashed up Bartlett's.'

'Coo! D'you see 'em?'

'My dad did. Coo – *wham*, it went, he said. They was all
buckled together . . . '

'Quiet, boys. I'd better put a nought in the register and
we must get on with some table practice.'

'Sometimes Patrick takes his dad's dinner up to him.
He's lambing over Dunnett's, and it takes a good half-hour
to get there.'

'Not if he goes Green Lane way.'

'Green Lane way! 'S'under water, soppy. He'd have to
cut up over the hill, and then it takes a good half-hour
easy. Don't it, Bill? Easy takes half-hour, I said, don't it?'

'I dunno. Never bin.'

'That'll do, children. The time we've wasted! All turn this way and stop this incessant chattering . . .'

'Miss, I've just thought! Patrick said his auntie was coming today.'

'That shouldn't stop him coming to school.'

'Ah, but she was coming to look after the little 'uns while Patrick's mum went to see their old grandma that was took to the hostipal . . .'

'Hospital!'

'Hostipal, that's right. So if she never come . . .'

'Didn't come.'

'. . . they would have to stay with Patrick, because they're only little, look, and they've only got a noil stove, the electric isn't up that far yet, and they wouldn't be safe like.'

'That's it, mate! You got it!'

'But you said you saw his mum shaking her mat. She'd have been waiting for the bus.'

'She'd still have time to catch it. Ted Brooks is on this week, and he'd wait a bit for her.'

'Did you hear what she was hollering?'

'Something about the cold. Here, I've just thought again! I bet she said "A cold"! I bet Patrick's got a cold. And Jane too. I bet that's it all right. I bet . . .'

'Boys, boys! No more about Patrick, please. I've closed the register, and that's that. Hands on ribs! Breathe in – out – in – out!'

Balked in their detective work, the children breathe fiercely, and their eyes become prominent.

There is a scuffling outside, the Gothic door crashes back into the nature table, and Patrick and Jane appear wild-eyed on the threshold.

'Overslept,' says he succinctly.

Goldfish and Frogspawn

In the corner of our schoolroom stands a marmalade-coloured cupboard, curiously grained with scrolls and whorls by some bygone painter's hand. It harbours all the awkward things that have no real home anywhere else. A set of massive wooden geometrical shapes is flung in here, with odd gym shoes, cricket stumps, some Victorian annuals noted for an alarming series called 'Happy Deathbed Scenes', a jostle of maps and modulators, and a distressing wall chart showing the effects of alcohol on the human heart. Every school, that is not hopelessly streamlined and soulless, has just such a cupboard, and it goes without saying that it is this one that important visitors open – and then close hastily, with a nervous laugh.

On top of this useful receptacle stands our fish tank. For over two years six goldfish gleamed and gobbled before the loving gaze of the class; but during the last few weeks their number has dwindled, and one by one, pathetic, limp corpses have had their glinting glory covered by the cold earth in the school garden. Last Monday morning the sole survivor was found, floating on his side, and there was universal lamentation.

'Poor ol' fish,' said Ernest, compassionately. 'Died of a

lonely heart, I shouldn't wonder.' Ernest is sentimental, and a keen reader of the 'Happy Deathbed' series, if given half a chance.

'Stummer-cake, more like,' said Richard, a realist. 'I see a dead fish once . . .'

'Never mind that now,' I said hastily. 'Fred, you'd better bury it at once.'

Fred Mobbs, who had been angling for the body with a wire strainer, carried his dripping burden tenderly away, followed by the sad graze of the mourners.

During the morning there were many glances at the top of the cupboard, and at intervals there would be a shattering sigh.

'Quiet, ain't it, without the fish?' remarked Richard, who was supposed to be writing a composition.

'Proper awful!' agreed his neighbour sombrely. Pens faltered to a stop, and somebody in the back row said:

'That tank don't look right, empty like that. Miss, couldn't we have some more fish?'

Twenty pairs of eyes looked hopefully at me. Twenty upturned faces pleaded. Twenty pens, I noticed, were laid quietly to rest. It was obvious that little work would be done in this aura of gloom unless some ray of hope lightened it.

'Let's have some frogspawn for a change,' I suggested. A wave of enthusiasm greeted this remark.

'There's masses up Dunnett's pond. Great, enormous masses . . .'

'More down our way, near the ford!'

'You try and get it, mate! All squishy up over your wellingtons where those ol' bullocks goes and drinks. Up Dunnett's now . . .'

'That ain't frogspawn, Miss. I see it. It's in long ropes,

that is . . . it's toadspawn, honest! It's poison! My grandma said . . .'

Information, wildly inaccurate, and more allied to witchcraft than natural history, was being bandied about the room.

'Bring some frogspawn any day this week,' I said finally, 'and the child who works most quietly now can clean out the fish tank.' Peace reigned.

Next morning, Ernest, Fred and Patrick were absent. The hands of the wall clock crept from nine to nine-thirty, and I had quite given them up, when the door burst open, crashing back into the nature table and setting its catkins and coltsfoot aquiver. The three were huddled over a huge saucepan which appeared to be awash with a piece of submerged chain-mail. They dumped their heavy burden on my desk, slopping water in all directions, and stood back, bright-eyed. Their clothes were wet, their boots odorous and slimy, and their hands were an appalling sight.

'We got it for you!' said the first.

'Frogspawn, Miss!' said the second.

'Wasn't half a job!' said the third. They exchanged proud glances, sniffing happily.

'And could I take the saucepan back now, Miss?' added Patrick.

'Won't it do at dinner-time? You're all very late, you know.'

Patrick twisted his black hands uncomfortably, and Ernest came to his aid.

'Miss, it's Patrick's mum's biggest saucepan, and she'll want it to boil a pig's head in this morning.'

'Good heavens! Does she know you've had it?' There

was a pricking silence. Fred Mobbs shuffled his feet and took up the tale.

'She was up the butcher's getting the pig's head when Patrick went to get something to put our frogspawn in. We was in the pond, Ern and me, holding the stuff while Patrick run home for something. It's horrible slippery, Miss, and weighs near a ton, and it kep' all on slipping back . . .' He faltered to a stop.

'If you let me take it home now, Miss,' said Patrick beseechingly, 'I'll run all the way, and she won't mind . . . well, not much,' he added, as a sop to common honesty, 'especially if I could take a little note explaining?' The three bedraggled adventurers looked at me, across their saucepan full of treasure. This, I decided, was no time for petty recriminations. We must all hang together.

'Put some water in the tank,' I directed, "while I write the note.' Beaming, they departed on their mission, while I sat down to compose a tactful letter of explanation.

The children had stopped work and were watching breathlessly, as Ernest, perched on a chair, leant over the fish tank, saucepan poised. With a satisfying splash the frogspawn glided in, swirled, sank, and rose again . . . as heartening a promise of spring as the blue and white violets on the window-sill. Our cupboard was crowned again.

Eight-a-Side Cricket

'Us boys is one short, Miss,' says Ernest, 'so we'd better have you, I suppose.'

'That's right,' I agree, ignoring the dying fall of this statement, as I rummage for stumps behind a pile of musty wallpaper books at the back of the cupboard.

We have eight girls and seven boys in the class, so that unless one of the girls is conveniently absent on games afternoon, I am invited, in a resigned way, to join the boys. I am one of the opening batsmen, as this not only gets me out of the way quickly, but leaves me free to umpire.

'Lead on, girls, and wait at the church gate.'

We always wait here, so that we can cross the road safely to Mr Roberts's field. The traffic consists, on Tuesday and Fridays, of the baker's van, which remains stationary outside the farm house for half an hour while Sid Stone, the driver, shares a pot of tea with his sister in the kitchen, an occasional tractor, and four Aylesbury ducks who use the middle of the lane for a dust bath. There is no point, however, in learning kerb drill if we do not put it into practice.

Once inside the field we get down to business. Kitty, the cart horse, is driven off the pitch into the outfield, we ram in the stumps, tear off surplus garments – the girls hanging theirs on the hawthorn hedge while the boys have to be restrained from slinging theirs down in the muddy patch by the gate – and then we toss.

Ernest wins, and elects that we boys should bat first, so David, a nine-year-old gypsy, and I drag our bats over the bumpy grass and take up our positions.

I catch sight of the layers of clothing still swaddling my partner. 'Why don't you take some of those jerseys off?' I shout down the pitch to him.

'Ain't 'ot!' he shouts back.

I give it up, and prepare to face Ann the bowler, who grips the ball in a menacing way as she places her field.

'Come on in,' she commands a shrinking Carol, who is a tender seven-year-old, with no front teeth, and weighs about three stone. 'If you're put mid-on you have to get up close! This ball don't hurt if you catches it right!'

I intervene. 'Put Carol at long-stop and let Beryl be mid-on.' It is doubtful if a cricket ball plumb on the thumb would have any galvanic action on the lethargic Beryl, and in any case she was reached the ripe old age of ten and has three cricket seasons behind her.

Ann now rushes up to the wicket, a welter of brown arms and pink gingham. The ball hits my bat and rolls a few yards away to a small molehill. As I step out to pat it down David yells, 'Come on!' as he flashes down towards me. I obey meekly and we run two. Fighting for breath I face the second ball.

'Don't be afraid to step right out to the ball,' I tell the children, doing so. My off stump lurches sickeningly.

'Treacle, Miss,' calls Ann, meaning I can have another turn.

'Treacle! That's treacle all right! You stay there, Miss,' shout both teams kindly. I refuse their handsome offer and give my bat to Ernest. He puts it between his knees, spits on his hands, grips the handle, and swaggers out to the wicket. He looks round at the eight girls with narrowed, supercilious eyes.

'Show off!' shouts Richard from the hedge. 'Thinks hisself a Bedser!'

Ann bowls. Ernest takes a tremendous swipe at it, and falls dramatically flat with his bat outstretched. Kitty, who has been grazing nearer and nearer, now stops midway between the wickets.

'That ol' horse . . .' snaps Ernest irritably, and both teams advance upon Kitty, who gazes at her young friends in a benign way. We are about to put our sixteen shoulders to her flank when Mr Roberts calls from the house and she ambles off.

'I'll bet those cricket chaps up at Lord's and that don't have no ol' horses on the pitch,' grumbles Ernest, picking up his bat.

'They don't even let 'em come in the outfield,' John tells him authoritatively.

Ann bowls again, Ernest skies it towards an ominous black cloud, and everyone shouts at the innocent Carol, who, with her back to the game, is waving energetically to someone in the next field.

'Look out! You're supposed to be playing cricket! Wasn't even turned this way!'

'I was only waving to my dad!' protests Carol. Further recriminations are cut short by a sharp spatter of hail.

'Collect your things quickly,' I call, 'and run in! Mind the road!' I bellow after them, as a gesture to our kerb drill. They straggle off, coats over heads, to escape the pitiless bombardment. Ernest and I wrestle with the stumps, and lumber after them.

With something like smugness in her mild eye, Kitty watches us go. Then she turns back to her own again.

Night and Day

'This,' I say, switching on the light, 'is the sun.'

The class looks at it with awe.

'And this,' I say, twirling the globe neatly with one finger on Alsaka, 'is the earth.'

There is a respectful silence. It is one of those taut moments packed with psychological importance, child wonder and the impact of knowledge.

The spell is broken by Alan, who asks in a fruity Berkshire voice, 'But it don't keep on turning, does it?'

'Does,' I correct automatically. 'Yes, it does. It never stops. Day and night, week after week.' I tell the children, 'it turns round and round and round; and just here, is Great Britain, where we live.'

The class stands up as one man, and I wave it down again. It is not easy to show the British Isles to a mob of eager children. Apart from its minute nature this country's peculiar position on the upper slopes of the globe make it necessary to carry the whole contraption round the class in a pointing position with the brass knob to the front.

Fellows of the Royal Geographical Society will have no difficulty in following my meaning.

Half the class say they can't see, while the other half tell the first half to sit down.

I put the globe back on the table and attempt to recapture dawning wonder. I point to the naked light bulb.

'There is the sun shining up in the sky. All the people who live here,' I stroke the class side of the globe seductively, 'are saying ' "What a lovely day!" ' '

I drop my voice about an octave.

'But who knows what the people on my side of the globe are saying?'

Silence.

'Well, will they be looking up at the sun?'

Silence becomes unhappy.

'Well, will they? Think! Will they be able to see the sun? John, tell me.'

John, cornered, says he don't know what they says. If they doeos say anything, he adds. But, in any case, he don't know.

I start all over again. The sun – heads tip up, the globe – heads tip forward, the seductive stroke – the people *in the sun*!

We are poised again.

'But what about the people on this side of the globe? Can they see the sun?'

Brian don't see why not if they are looking. He is ignored.

Jane says reasonably that all of them as is on her side of the globe is in the sun because the electric is switched on.

I agree. Now we are getting warmer.

'Well, then, if all the people facing the light are in the sun, what are the other people doing?'

Deadlock again.

I begin to go mad. I stick a pin into the steppes of Russia and revolve the globe again with horrible deliberation.

'Here I am,' I say with emphasis, touching the pin, 'and I am just waking up. I can see the sun rising. Now it's the afternoon, now it's the evening. Are you *watching*? It's beginning to get dark. Now it really is dark. Tell me, is it still the daytime?'

'*No!*' A lusty Berkshire roar.

'Where am I now?'

'Round the back!'

Fair enough. Not what the Royal Geographical Society would care to hear, probably, but we progress.

'What am I doing now, then?'

They tell me I be in the dark, I be in bed, it be the night and the day be over.

We smile triumphantly at each other, glowing with effort rewarded and flushed with new knowledge.

I twirl the globe dizzily. The pin flies round and round, and we shout 'DAY – NIGHT' and feel terrific.

'Now,' I tell the class with conviction, 'you really do know what causes the day and night.'

'Yes,' says Jane happily, 'switching on the electric.'

The Runaway

It was very quiet in the infants' room. The score of children sat in their pygmy armchairs engrossed in making Plasticine baskets. The initial rapture of making long sinuous worms, by rubbing the lovely stuff back and forth under their hot palms, was over. Now the coiling process was in operation, although one or two slap-dash basket-makers had already twirled theirs up, and had to be exhorted to further efforts to keep them occupied.

'And now you can fill the basket with vegetables, carrots and turnips, for instance.'

'Potatoes are easier,' pointed out one lazy child.

'The end of my basket handle will do for a cucumber,' said an even lazier one, tossing it in nonchalantly.

The afternoon was warm and conducive to torpor. One or two zealous infants had set themselves such formidable tasks as cabbage-making, but on the whole potatoes, and other globular vegetables which could be made with a twirl or two of the forefinger, were more popular. The door was propped open and the drowsy sound of the vicar's lawn mower and a nearby wood pigeon could be

heard. It seemed to be that this dreamy peace could never be shattered. I was mistaken.

At one of the low tables in the front of the classroom sat a thin, quiet child. He had fine, wispy hair, watery eyes and a receding chin. He wore a cotton shirt, obviously cut down from an adult garment, thick tweed trousers supported by braces, and a pair of minute black plimsolls. He was the unobtrusive sort of child that never needs to be scolded, lacking in mischief and vitality. In his hand he held a long strip of Plasticine which he appeared to be eating with the greatest relish. Thoughts of common hygiene, sickness and, I must admit, the usual shortage of Plasticine prompted me to speak more sharply than usual.

'Don't eat that!' I rapped out.

The child looked up, startled. His small mouth dropped open, revealing shreds of green material adhering to his pink tongue. Then, in one bound, he leapt to his feet, overturning his armchair.

'I shall go home!' he exclaimed, with the utmost emphasis. And in a flash he was through the open door.

To say that we were flabbergasted is an understatement. We remained stiff with shock, caught like so many flies in amber. I was the first to recover.

'Stay there!' I ordered the gaping class, and set off in pursuit.

I could see the runaway legging it towards the village in fine style. For a weakly child with legs not much stouter than willow sticks he covered the ground at a remarkable speed. I pounded after him, impeded by a voluminous skirt which clung maddeningly round my legs. It was fruitless to call to the child, I decided, tearing past the farm gate and frightening severely two cows who had been gazing over it. I might just as well save my failing breath for running.

'Getting your weight down?' called a facetious fellow, over a hedge. The child, by this time, had vanished round the corner by the butcher's shop. I did not deign to answer, but tried to increase my speed. Heavens! What an awful lung-searing business running was! Bannister, Pirie, Ibbotson . . . heroes all of them, I thought jerkily. Now I had a stone in my shoe. Never mind, think of that poor fellow who ran all the way from somewhere to somewhere with a thorn in his foot to bring the news of something or other. The blood thumped in my head as I turned the corner by the butcher's. There, many yards ahead, sped the horrible child, his black plimsolls twinkling, but my spirits rose, for a little farther on a cottage was being rethatched, and I could see the thatcher, from his perch on the roof, was watching the child with interest. His mate was runtling among a welter of straw in the tiny front garden. I gathered my flagging resources for one final effort.

'Stop – that – child!' I wheezed imploringly, wondering if the valves of my heart would ever be the same again. With maddening deliberation the man in the garden straightened up. Slowly he raised his eyes to his lofty companion.

'What say?' he drawled.

'Stop that kid!' bellowed the thatcher, and miraculously his mate looked over the hedge. He leapt over the straw, through the gate, and caught the runaway in his out-stretched arms.

When I arrived I found the child quiescent and uncon-cerned. He had had a pleasant run and seemed to have forgotten the cause of it. Too breathless to do more than thank the men I took the boy by the hand and we returned, amicably and silently, to school. What chaos I should find there I did not dare to think.

We crossed the threshold hand in hand. To my amaze-ment, the class still sat in stupefied silence. The child returned to his desk, and vegetable modelling continued generally. I looked at the clock and saw that exactly six minutes had passed since embarking on our escapade.

As I cooled down and the sound of the vicar's lawn mower and the nearby wood pigeon returned, a sudden appalling thought shattered me. What was there to stop any of the children from rushing from the room, now or at any time, for that matter? What could a teacher do when faced with a mass escape? It could happen with dangerous ease. Perhaps prevention would be better than future races round the village.

'Roll up your Plasticine,' I said. 'I want to speak to you.'

Borrow a Pound

'Seven from three you can't!
'Borrow a ten!' chants the middle row.

'A what?'

'A *ten*!'

The six children in the row by the fish tank look superior and exchange secret smiles. They constitute the top group, and have left such childish things as £ *s. d.* long ago.

The four children in the bottom group stop scrabbling over their lowly boxes of figures and look up hopefully. You never know, I may fly off the handle again and that is always a pleasant diversion.

'Look again. What are you dealing with?'

'Seven from three,' uncertainly.

'Yes, but seven whats? Three whats?'

After a time Ernest says he don't see why it shouldn't be money really, as us had got £ *s. d.* on the blackboard like.

The rest of the middle row look apprehensive. This is the sort of remark that often touches me off.

'This boy has more sense than the rest of you put together. I can always rely on Ernest to think things out.'

Relief floods the room, and it is obvious that Ernest will be left to carry on the good work. The bottom group turn back to their boxes with disappointed faces. No fireworks.

'Very well. What are you going to borrow if you are dealing with shillings?'

'A shilling.'

'Don't shout. How can the others work if you make that terrible noise?'

The children on each side look important and apply themselves with much heavy breathing and writhing of tongues.

'You have told me that you can't take seven shillings from three shillings, so you must borrow something. What?'

There is a perplexed silence.

'Would it be a ten?' hazards John.

'Or a one?' suggests Ann.

'I reckons you gets pence if you borrows anything. Which would be twelvses,' says Peter decidedly.

'You're borrowing from the wrong column,' I point out. 'Borrow from the left-hand one, then what do you get?'

'A pound!' A united roar.

'How many shillings?'

'Twenty!' Only half the volume this time.

'You don't seem very sure. Everyone?'

'*Twenty!*'

A bee disturbed by the uproar buzzes out from the window-sill and circles the boxes of figures angrily. All three groups converge upon the intruder with rulers, pencil boxes, and (a very few) handkerchiefs raised.

'All right, all right. Go back at once. Leave the thing

alone and it won't hurt you.' The hubbub continues, and I raise my voice above the din.

'First row back goes out to play first!'

Peace reigns. Arms are folded fiercely, hobnails stand decorously side by side, and the only sound is made by the rescued bee.

'All very nice, early play for the whole class. Now for this sum. Twenty shillings we'll borrow, then.'

'I reckons you don't need all them shillings,' objects Peter. 'Ten would be enough!'

'I agree, but I must take one unit from this column, and the unit is a pound note. That makes twenty for the shilling column. I can't take less than one, can I?'

A discontented muttering from Peter.

'Speak up, boy. What's worrying you?'

'I'd 'ave took a ten-shilling note,' persists Peter.

'And a pretty pass you'd be in when you reached the pound column,' I tell him flatly, turning round to the board impatiently. 'Now, seven from twenty-three?'

'Fifteen,' says Ernest promptly. I write it up thankfully. Dear old Ernest, always reliable.

''Taint! 'Tis sixteen!' bellows Peter triumphantly, and I think I see his tongue flash out at Ernest as I stoop for the duster.

'You did ought to 'ave borrowed a ten-shillng note,' Peter continues sententiously, 'like I said, Miss. You'd 'ave found it come easier.'

The Flag

Three times a day, for almost the whole of the week, the boys' playground at the village school had presented a scene of intense martial activity. At morning playtime, during the dinner-hour and throughout the afternoon break all the males, from five to eleven, had rushed together, the minute they had burst from the classrooms, and had milled round and round seething with excitement.

Perhaps not quite all the males . . . for a few very tender babies, still tied resentfully to the apron strings of aggressive older sisters, stayed on their own side of the iron railings gazing longingly at the turmoil on the other and ready to slip over the minute that their sisters' attention was engaged elsewhere. In theory, all the little boys under seven should have been here with the girls, playing such decorous games as hide and seek and marbles, but most of them had already broken bounds to join the riot next door.

After the initial uproar some order became apparent. A large new Union Jack was hoisted by one of the bigger boys, a fat freckled child with a voice like a foghorn. This last attribute had doubtless led to his present position of eminence and he was treated with the greatest respect by the smaller fry. His booming voice sounded above their shriller notes like Big Ben above the traffic, and before long the crowd broke into two groups. Each child carried a stick of some sort, sloped over his shoulder like a gun. They ranged from slender ash sticks, gleaming dully like rods of pewter, to chunky pieces of old desks which had been stacked for years in a cobwebby corner behind the shed.

The fat boy hoisted the flag, on its bean pole, and set off for the coke bunker, a red brick building which stood at the top of the sloping playground. He was followed by a single file of martial figures. 'Left – right – left – right!' boomed the flag bearer, and the fact that most of his band were marching right – left – right – left did not diminish the military effect.

At the same time the rest set off downhill, following their leader, a tall, lanky boy in torn grey trousers. On his left arm was tied a red ribbon which had once adorned a chocolate box. One might have thought him recently vaccinated but for the violent rallying gestures which he gave his followers, combined with ferocious exhortations in an assumed foreign tongue.

At the bottom of the playground ran a grassy ditch, and here the band hid themselves, ranging their wooden fire-arms across the parapet and squinting murderously along them to the distant Union Jack which crowned the coal bunker above a jostle of tousled heads. After a few moments one child would emerge and advance stealthily from the ditch to the dustbin, where he would take cover, then from the dustbin to a buttress at the side of the school, and from the buttress to the flimsy protection of a prunus tree. Here he would stop and signal to the watchers in the ditch, who poured forth, yelling blue murder. At the same time the Union Jack party leapt from the top of the crunching coke, equally vociferous, and the two sides met in joyous combat.

Watching this game from the staff room window I meant to inquire just what it was all about. I assumed, naturally enough, that it was inspired by one of the more stirring episodes in our British history. Could it be the Civil Wars? Or Kitchener at Khartoum perhaps? Or the Siege of Lucknow? Certainly the flag seemed to play an important part and it was heartening to see that patriotism still burnt brightly in some places. Of course, as soon as I returned to the pressing problems of the classroom I forgot all about it, and on my duty day I was so delighted to have the boys wholesomely occupied in organized combat rather than the normal innumerable private fights that I spent a pleasurable time among the girls for a change.

Friday came. The game was still enthralling, the boys tearing from the classroom gulping down the last of their elevenses and with their mouths ringed with wet milk. Today I really must find out which part of our island story I had seen enacted all the week. It might be Romans and Britons, of course, I told myself, clanging over the door scraper into a fine drizzle; or Picts and Scots, or Alfred and the Danes. Alfred, they had been told, had been born, and had fought too, not far from their own village.

The two armies were marching resolutely away from each other and I caught the last man in the Union Jack party.

'What's the game?' I asked.

'The game?' he repeated, looking shocked.

'With the flag,' I said, pointing to it as it fluttered valiantly at the end of its bean pole, 'and the two armies.'

His face cleared.

'Oh that!' he said. 'Why, Yank Cavalry and Indians!'

And setting his wooden gun more securely on his shoulder he set off across the arid Arizonian wastes of a wet Berkshire playground.

Lost Property

The procession began during scripture lesson. The story of Joseph, as colourful and engrossing as ever, was being unwound before my attentive class when the door first opened. It stumped a thick-set infant dangling a navy-blue raincoat belt. Ignoring me, she held it up, snake-like, to the class.

'Anyone lost this off of their raincoat?' she piped in a voice shrill with importance.

'"Off" or "from",' I corrected automatically aloud. '"His" or "her",' I added silently to myself. I felt unequal to explaining it all to the child, particularly as Joseph was in the midst of recounting his first dream to a decidedly unfavourable audience.

'I said, "Off of"!' protested the child indignantly. I felt even less keen to embark on a grammar lesson on the side, as it were, and anxious to return to Joseph.

My class looked with lack-lustre eyes upon the raincoat belt, but no one spoke.

'Make sure, now!' I rallied them. 'It may be yours!'

'Not mine, Miss.'

'I've got mine all right!'

'Belongs to that new girl, don't it?'

'What new girl? Down our end?'

'No, no! That girl in Miss Whatsername's. You know, with the hair.'

This cryptic exchange had evidently meant more to our visitor than to me for she was already setting off for the door trailing the belt behind her. A few papers fluttered to the floor as the door shut, and after picking them up we resumed our lessons. We had just got Joseph comfortably off on his journey to the vale of Hebron when the door opened again. A small child, flaunting a large and distressingly grubby handkerchief like a flag, stood before us.

'Anyone's?' I rapped out, before the child could speak.

'No,' chorused the class. The child retreated before the roar.

'And at last,' I said, 'he came within sight of his brothers.' The class wriggled pleasurably and settled down again. 'But while Joseph was still a long way off his brothers began to plot against him . . . '

Someone fumbled at our door handle. We ignored the rattling and I pressed on.

The rattling became urgent and a faint piping, as of some distant moorhen in distress, was added to the disturbance.

'See who it is,' I said resignedly.

Tutting exasperatedly, the nearest boy flung back the door, almost capsizing a minute creature who was struggling with an outsize pair of wellingtons clutched against his chest.

'These was in our cloakroom,' he gasped fearfully. He advanced uncertainly into the room, tripping over the milk crate as he came. The noise was insupportable.

'For pity's sake,' I roared above the din, 'put those things down and look where you're going!'

The poor child put the wellingtons down obediently and turned to face the amused gaze of his elders.

'Anybody's wellingtons?' I queried with what patience I could muster. 'Look hard, now. And think!'

'No, Miss!' came the chorus again. The wispy child picked up his burden again and staggered out.

'Now, where were we?'

'Joseph's brothers, Miss. Plotting, Miss.' I took up the oft-snapped thread again.

'They were so wickedly jealous by this time that they planned to kill Joseph. One of them remembered a deep pit near by, and he said . . .'

A hand wavered aloft in the back row.

'You can wait,' I said. 'And he suggested to the others that they should throw Joseph's body into the deep pit, where it would lie hidden.' The children's eyes grew rounder and their gaze more intent. Still that annoying hand remained aloft. To its silent appeal was added a verbal one.

'Miss, them wellingtons.'

'Well, what about them?'

'They were mine, Miss. I've just thought.' The class sighed, and turned round to look at the wretched boy with a disgust which equalled my own.

'Go and get them,' I said, dangerously quiet, 'and don't come back until I've finished this story.'

He slunk from the room and I continued doggedly.

'But Reuben, who was much more kind-hearted than his

brothers, thought of a better plan. He knew that his old father would be dreadfully sad if anything happened to Joseph . . .'

The door burst open again with an explosive crack. It was not, as I first thought, the luckless owner of the wellingtons returning, thereby adding flagrant disobedience to his other vices, but a beaming boy carrying a brown paper carrier bag with great care. And what might that contain, I mused? A lost train set? Five hundred pieces of jigsaw puzzle? Fourteen gym shoes – all odd?

He stopped beside my desk, still smiling importantly and quite oblivious of the bottled rage that seethed so near him. He held out the carrier bag.

'Would you like to show your class . . .' he said. I cut him short.

'Anybody own . . .' I began, thrusting my hand hastily into the cavernous depths. I stopped with a yelp. Inside, tightly curled up, was a hedgehog.

PT for Forty

Now let me see who is ready for PT. It's such a lovely sunny morning I think you can take your frocks off, girls.

Boys, take off jackets and waistcoats and any jerseys. Hang them on the back of your chairs.

That's the way, Anna, plenty of fresh air, that's what our bodies need. Well, if you've got a cold, Elsie, you can just tuck your frock in your knickers today, but take off your cardigan.

Mummy said not to?

Now look, dear, you'll get so hot jumping and running in the playground and then when you come in here again you'll get cool, so that you must have something to put on. Take it off, like Anna.

Oh, don't cry, child! Look at all these other children, half-naked some of them, and as jolly as sand-boys!

That's right. That looks much better.

All ready? Lead to the door.

As soon as you get into the playground I want to see some nice, high, galloping horses. When I blow my whistle change into bouncing balls.

Lead on, Jane and Richard. Don't push, Michael.

Fetch my coat, dear, will you? The wind's rather chilly.

What lovely horses! Up, up, up! That's the way.

Who didn't hear the whistle? You're all supposed to be balls now.

Right. All rest.

Now this time I want big, high, bouncing balls. Sixpenny ones – those were only penny ones I saw just now.

Right up as high as the trees! Up, up, up! Lovely!

Everybody quite still. Pull up as tall as you can.

Into a big circle. Run.

Don't pull, Michael; just hold hands nicely. John, stop pushing in; find a space!

All drop hands. There's no need to wrench each others' arms half out every time we make a circle!

All run away again.

Back to a circle. That's better, though I can still see some rough people, Michael.

Down to touch toes, down. Keep those knees pressed back. Push, push, push. Lovely!

Up again.

All stretch up as tall as a house. Higher still!

Now as small as a mouse. Tuck your heads in and squeeze up as small as you can. It's no good sticking your legs out at the back, Jane, mice don't do that. Tuck them up.

Now as wide as a gate. Stretch those arms sideways, but mind your neighbour, John Todd.

Now as thin as a pin. Straight backs, heads up, pull those stomachs in!

I can see some lovely pins.

As tall as a house! Lovely!

As small as a mouse! Much better!

As wide as a gate! Very good!

As thin as a pin! Beautiful pins!

Girls, run and fetch a hoop each and see how long you can keep it up. Try not to bump into anyone.

Boys, you are going to have a ball each. I want you to practise throwing it up and catching it. Play with your ball on this side of the playground. We don't want to send any into Mrs Parker's garden, do we?

Off you go, then.

I can see some really clever little girls with hoops.

Very nice, boys, but not too high, and keep *away from that fence*, Peter.

There now. Well, you'll just have to go round and knock at Mrs Parker's door, Peter. It's no use crying, you could have played where you were told.

Last time she said what?

She never wanted to see you again? I'm not surprised.

Oh, come now, cheer up. Dry your eyes and go round, Peter.

Get on with your hoops and balls, the rest of you!

Say you are very sorry but your ball is in her garden and may you fetch it.

Yes, yes, I know what Mrs Parker said, but it's your duty to go. There are a great many unpleasant things in this life, dear, that just have to be faced. Now go along.

Richard, what on earth has happened? All stand still.

Michael pushed you over? Come here, Michael. Look at this poor child's knees. Aren't you ashamed?

You are a thoroughly naughty little boy, Michael. Go and stand by my desk.

Let me look, Richard.

Oh, dear!

Anna, take him in. Fetch some cottonwool from the first-aid box and some lint, please – oh, and scissors. Perhaps I can find a sweet in my cupboard, Richard. You're being a very brave boy.

The rest of you hold up balls and hoops.

Girls, tiptoe to the wall and put back your hoops, then stand on the white line.

Boys, *quietly* put the balls away, then *creep* to the other white line.

All as thin as a pin! Lovely!

Lead on, children.

There's going to be a sweet for any child who can dress and sit in its desk without saying *one word*!

Clerical Error

Shoulder high, round two sides of the playground, runs a Cotswold wall of dry stone. Here and there it is saddled with heavy swags of ivy, attractive not only to the bees and birds, but also to the children who use the leaves for plates, fans, money and other paraphernalia of their games. Sometimes long, bitter-smelling ropes are torn away to tie up a prisoner, but the wall and the ivy have suffered no real damage until this week.

I first saw the mess at the end of playtime. A heap of stones lay scattered at the foot of the wall. They had fallen from a large, ragged gap at the top, near some ivy, and it was obvious that someone would have to spend an hour or two setting the wall to rights again.

'How did it happen?' I asked the children, when they were sitting, looking sheepish, in their desks.

An unhappy silence fell, broken only by a nervous cough from John, who takes all the cares of the world upon himself.

'Well, come along!' I encouraged them. I looked at David, who is usually mixed up in little matters like this.

'I wasn't there!' he said hastily, like Pooh-Bah, on another awkward occasion.

John coughed again and said huskily, 'We was only playing.' His fingers wove together ceaselessly.

'Who?'

At this, John looked at his feet, the other children looked at John, and the room grew very still.

While we were thus caught, motionless, the bell which hangs by the school door, attached to a long cord, began

to peal deafeningly, frightening the wits out of all of us.

'The vicar,' said Anne, hastening to the door. No one else ever hauls on our bell-pull with quite such prolonged vigour. The children exchanged looks and smiles. Relief, I told myself, from the last few minutes' tension.

'I see the wall's down,' said the vicar. 'Anyone hurt?'

'No,' I answered, 'I'm just making a few inquiries.'

'Oh!' said the vicar, and turned to the class with a cheerful bellow.

'Anyone know anything about it?'

There was some uncomfortable shuffling. Faces grew red and eyes were downcast. Even Eric, an irrepressible chatterbox, had nothing to say, but began to blow his nose fussily.

The vicar turned back again.

'Can't stop. Meeting at four . . . but we'll get the wall up again by the end of the week. Here's the hymn list.' And with a flutter of ecclesiastical coat tails he had gone.

Eric removed his handkerchief and I saw that he was laughing. Squeaks and giggles from other parts of the room began to echo his mirth.

'This,' I began, with some hauteur, 'is no laughing matter. I should prefer a little common honesty over this damage to school property.'

'But Miss,' said John earnestly, owl-eyed among his quivering friends, 'us never had no chance to tell you.'

'Why not?'

'Because of the vicar, Miss. That was what we was playing.'

'That's right!' agreed Anne.

'All the little 'uns was in the old desk in the playground, being in school, and I was beating them with a stick and hollering at them, because I was . . . well, I was the teacher, see . . .' He began to falter.

I decided to let this outrageous comment on my teaching methods go by unchallenged.

'Well, what else? That doesn't account for the wall.'

'It do really, Miss, because Eric was the vicar, and came calling, and he give a good old pull on the bell rope . . . that was the ivy, Miss . . . and it just sort of crumbled away, didn't it, Eric?

Eric, however, was past corroboration, being in that happy state of near-hysteria which catches one so gloriously in the ribs in youth.

Above the general uproar John's solemn voice pursued me relentlessly.

'So when the vicar asked us who done it, what could we say? We couldn't say the vicar done it, because he didn't really; although Eric was the vicar in the game, and he done it, but only because he had to be like the real vicar. And we couldn't tell the real vicar we was playing at being vicar . . .'

'John,' I begged,'Please, that's quite enough. All is forgiven. The incident is closed.'

Afterglow

The schoolroom door is propped open with an upturned flowerpot. The children, sprawling damply in their desks, stare at the blisters forming on the faded paint and look forward to popping them at playtime.

'Copy "Coronation Day" from the blackboard,' I direct, 'and then we'll see how much you can remember.'

Languidly they reach for their pens and scratch the bottoms of the ink-wells. Composition lesson is never popular, and the combination of recent village celebrations and the scorching heat makes the effort of thought almost impossible.

John unsticks one hot leg and presses it luxuriously against the cold iron upright of his desk. Richard is busy blowing down the front of his shirt. Even Edward, the head boy, wilts. His arms are stretched at full length across his desk, palms uppermost.

'Sit up, children,' I urge. 'Richard, what did you do on Coronation Day?'

He looks up defensively from his blowing.

'Never did nothing!' he says truculently.

'But you must have done something. Got up, for instance.'

'No, I never, Miss. I was took bad after the Cubs' supper the night before.'

I turn to Edward.

'That's right, Miss. I went to the Cub's supper too, and the vicar gave us all a Coronation penknife.'

'They's absolute smashers!' corroborates David, who is fiddling with something in his ink-well.

'Then that could go in your composition. But tell me something about the day itself.'

'It was lovely,' breathes Ann dreamily.

'Best Coronation I ever saw,' agrees seven-year-old John decidedly.

'It's certainly something you will always remember,' I say. 'David, throw away that horrid blob of whatever-it-is you've finished out of your ink-well into the basket!'

He obeys with a martyred sigh.

'And now, let's hear what you did on Coronation Day.'

'Helped tie lace curtains over our blackcurrant bushes.'

'And after that?'

'Topped and tailed goosegogs.'

'Can you remember anything to do with the Coronation?'

His brow clouds, and he rubs a glistening palm up and down his jacket front as he thinks.

'Afternoon,' he says at last, 'us all went up the rec. to have the tea.'

At this magic word, animation flickers for the first time through the hot room. Hubbub breaks out.

'Us ate nine cakes each!'

'My lemonade went all over my new frock!'

'Us could do with an ice or two now, eh, John?'

'Ah! Betcher!'

I raise a protesting hand and torpidity reigns again.

'Who heard the service on the wireless? Or saw it televised?'

A few moist hands flutter aloft.

'Then that can go in your composition. Can you think of anything else?'

'Old Mr Pettitt,' volunteers Ann at length, 'planted a silver birch up the rec. because he's the oldest man in the village.'

'That's a very good point. We shall all remember Coronation Day, when we see the birch tree growing. But, David . . .' He looks up wonderingly. 'Watch your spelling of "birch", please. I had quite enough "brids" and "grils" and "stroms" in your last composition.'

He looks aggrieved at this attack, and I turn back to the class.

'Any more ideas?'

Far away a cuckoo calls. The pinks on the window-sill, packed as tight as a cauliflower, send down heady waves of scent. The children sit bemused, their minds a happy confusion of sunshine, flags, music and a great glory somewhere . . . felt, but dimly comprehended. As for writing it down . . .

'You can start,' I say. 'Just do your best.'

The pen-chewing, sighing and scratching begin. Slowly the pages fill as I wander up and down the quiet room. I stop to read David's grubby effort. After twenty minutes' work his recollections of the day are summed up in one short, but triumphant sentence.

It says: 'I was the frist to crav my name on the new brich tree up the reck.'

Soft and Hard Boiled

'Well may you weep!' I said severely to the youngest of the three malefactors. She stood about a yard high and felt dismally in her knicker leg for her handkerchief. Tears coursed down her face in fat drops.

Mr Henry, the farmer, on whose behalf I was doing justice, began to weave unhappily about the schoolroom.

He stands six feet four in his gum-boots, played full back for the county for years, halts mad bulls with one hand and has a heart as soft as a marshmallow. I could see I should have trouble with him if I didn't hurry up the proceedings.

He was gazing miserably at a case of cocoa from 'Pod' to 'Dessert Chocolate'.

'Look,' he said desperately, approaching my desk, 'let them off this time.'

He spoke in what he thought was a whisper, but half a dozen tracings of South America were blown to the floor. He winced at the sight of the three children standing in front of the assembled school (all twenty-five of them).

The second child, seeing his harrowed face, now began to pipe her eye with some energy.

'Sorry I ever brought it up,' he muttered. 'Poor little things! So small –' His voice broke.

'Nonsense!' I said firmly. 'Not so small that they don't know right from wrong.'

I walked deliberately to the cupboard at the end of the classroom. There was a respectful hush. Tradition had it that there was a cane in that cupboard – never used, but much venerated. This was an Occasion.

I felt among the enormous wooden cones, cubes, hexagons and other massive shapes that these children's grandparents used to use for some mysterious bygone lesson.

Where was that dratted cane, I fumed to myself, with my head among the raffia?

'It's by them maps, Miss,' murmured the head boy, who should go far when he leaves school. He intends, he tells me, to work up the Atomic. I retrieved the cane from between the Holy Land and Muscles of the Human Body.

Mr Henry was nearly in tears himself when I put it on my desk.

'I shan't use it, silly,' I hissed at him with my back to the class, but I raised it solemnly and pointed it at the biggest sinner. He was of gipsy stock and wore long black corduroy

trousers, five jerseys, two waistcoats and a spotted neckerchief.
His round black eyes met mine
boldly.

'Abraham, you knew it was
wrong to take Mr Henry's eggs?'

'Yes, Miss.'

'And you knew, too, Anne?'

'Yes,' she sniffed remorsefully.

'And Carol?'

The smallest one nodded
dumbly. Her knicker leg had
failed to yield a handkerchief.

Mr Henry, I was glad to see, had pulled himself together and managed a creditably reproving shake of the
head.

'If this happens again,' I told the children, 'I shall use
this cane, not just show it to you.'

The school looked approving. Right's right, after all.

'How many eggs did you take, Carol?'

'One.'

'Then you will have one tap with this cane if you steal
again.'

I turned to Anne.

'I took free,' she said.

'Then you know how many taps you would get.'

I could feel the atmosphere relaxing. The end was in
sight. Mr Henry had seen justice done, the cane would
return to its dusty habitat and the Occasion was rounding
off nicely.

I pointed the cane at Abraham.

'I took a 'ole 'atful,' he said.

Mr Henry snorted, and began to blow his nose fussily.

'But I never went to the 'en 'ouse, Miss,' pleaded

Abraham, a heart-breaking gipsy whine creeping into his voice. 'They was all together, Miss – honest, Miss – atween the 'edge and the tractor shed.'

Mr Henry wheeled round delightedly.

'Well, what do you make of that?' he exclaimed, rummaging energetically in his breeches pocket. 'That's a real sharp lad! We've been scouring the place for weeks for that pullet's nest!'

Last Day of Term

The wastepaper basket is pressed down and running over. Two cupboards stand open, displaying neat piles of atlases, nature readers and history text-books, all with determinedly gay colours . . . the sugar coating the pill.

On a lower shelf are ranged most of the children's exercise books, much more shabby and sober than the books above. At the long side desk two boys have the happy and noisy task of ripping out the few clean sheets left in the almost finished exercise books and making a pile of rough paper ready for next term's tests. The ancient cupboard by the door has been left till last. This is the one that the children call 'the muck cupboard' because the odds and ends are stored here. It is cold and damp. A musty odour creeps forth whenever it is opened, redolent of the tombs which stand close by in the churchyard. Here we keep the clay tin, the chaotic bundle of raffia and the small children's sand trays We also keep, I suspect, mice; and when I have occasion to visit the cupboard I rattle the knob in a cowardly way so that any bright-eyed creatures within may vanish before I thrust in a trembling hand for the raffia.

The upper shelf has been tidied. Our vases are ranged in size from the gargantuan pink and green 'ark pot' as the children call it, through jam jars covered with stamps, Virol jars and earthenware honey pots down to minute fish paste jars used for wild violets and daisies. Below them two well-patched flannel trouser seats are displayed, as Peter and John tuck wet sacking over the balls of clay. 'Really soaking,' I say. 'It's got to stay moist for over five weeks!' The hubbub is intensified at this joyful thought. Desk lids crash up and down, children trot back and forth to the creaking wastepaper basket and the clatter of paint pots being washed outside in the venerable stone sink adds to the din. I go round the walls, prising out drawing-pins and handing out dusty pictures, painted by the class, to the rightful owners. Suddenly, there seems nothing more to do. The cupboard doors are shut, the walls are bare and the children settle in their empty desks. 'School starts again,' I tell them, 'on September the seventh. It's a Tuesday.' There are rustles and smiles. September! Think of that . . . months away! No more sitting on a hard wooden bench, clutching a stiff pen and watching the pigeons in the vicarage elms through the school window! But instead freedom! Grass to roll in, flowers to pick and trees to climb . . . five whole weeks in which to tear about in the the sun or loiter in the shade; to help dig potatoes or to steal a warm pod of peas from the row; to shout into the wind or to dream in the sun; to work or to play just as it suits you!

The church clock strikes four. The children stand to sing their grace. Some clutch bunches of wilting flowers between their hands, for to take home 'flowers from school' is something they love to do. These ageing blossoms rank much higher in their estimation then the fresh beauties that pack their own gardens. Their voices are shrill this afternoon, and in the four short lines of music they rise half a tone sharp with suppressed excitement. 'Good afternoon, children. Have a good holiday, and we'll meet again on September the seventh!'

'Good afternoon, Miss,' they carol. 'Good afternoon, I hope you have a nice holiday. I'll send you a card if I go to the sea. I'll bring you back some rock. Goodbye, Miss, goodbye!' They clatter out; the door crashes behind them; and a rose petal blows across the floor in the breeze.

It is very quiet in the schoolroom. I can hear the pigeons

plainly now from the vicarage garden, and there is a stealthy rustling from the cupboard. Can it possibly be a mouse I wonder for the hundredth time, or simply the raffia stirring in its confining skein? Resolutely, I turn the keys in the locks.

At the door I turn back for a final glance. The calendar, which we have forgotten to put away, stares back at me – 30 July it says. The next time I see it, it will proclaim 7 September, I think, as I unlock my desk and put the calendar on top of the register and hymn book. The elms will have started to drop a yellow leaf or two. There will be dahlia, not rose, petals on the floor, and the children will bring offerings of mushrooms and blackberries instead

of strawberries and raspberries carried carefully in handle-less cups. But all that is weeks away, I tell myself, as I finally lock up. The sun scorches my back as I turn the massive key in the school door. Swinging it jauntily round my finger, I go, whistling, to hang it up for five glorious weeks in its secret hiding-place at the back of the coalshed.